Campfire Stories

DATE DUE

OC 25 '00			
JY 15 '0			
NO 12 '02			
OC 16 '03			
JU 6 '0			
AP 0 '0			
MY 21 '0			

Campfire Stories

... things that go bump
in the night.

William W. Forgey, M.D.

Globe Pequot Press
Old Saybrook, Connecticut

CAMPFIRE STORIES

Copyright © 1985 by William W. Forgey, M.D.

ıy be reproduced or transmitted in any form
.cluding photocopying and recording, or by
m, except as may be expressly permitted by
ɛr. Requests for permission should be made
Box 833, Old Saybrook, Connecticut 06475.

Printed in the U.S.A.

1st Printing 5-85, 2nd Printing 4-87,
3rd Printing 11-87, 4th Printing 11-88,
5th Printing 3-89, 6th Printing 11-89,
7th Printing 11-92, 8th Printing 6-93,
9th Printing 5-94, 10th Printing 3-95
11th Printing 7-96, 12th Printing 4-98
13th Printing 5-99

Library of Congress Cataloging in Publication Data

Forgey, William W., 1942-
    Campfire stories.

    Bibliography: p.
    Summary: A collection of twenty ghost stories by a variety of authors with suggestions on how each should be told to a group, preferably around a campfire.
    1. Ghost stories, American. [1. Ghosts--Fiction.
2. Short stories]   I. Title.
PZ5.F75Cam 1985   [Fic]   85-2429
ISBN 0-934802-23-8

DEDICATION

This book is dedicated to Mike and Sid Nickels of Camp Palawopec, Nashville, Indiana.[1]

Mike and his wife Sid are special people. Staff and campers return year after year to the friendly, beautiful woodland setting of Camp Palawopec for many reasons -- but the primary reason is Mike and Sid.

There is adventure at Camp Palawopec. There is camaraderie and sports and beautiful woodlands. There are even campfires with stories. And I am fortunate to have been there to tell a few.

[1] Camp Palawopec, Box 172, R.R. 4, Nashville, Indiana 47448

ACKNOWLEDGEMENTS

My exposure to story telling has been because of my three scout troops and later to many of my friends while camping and canoeing. I appreciate their enthusiasm for more and more stories over the years.

I gratefully recognize the research and editorial assistance of Mark Szuster, a fellow wilderness traveler, who took time away from his studies to assist with this book.

The author also extends his thanks for permission to reprint the following copyrighted material:

To Macmillan of Canada, A Division of Gage Publishing Limited, to reprint "Nemesis" from *Tales of an Empty Cabin*, copyright 1936 by Grey Owl.

To Viking Penguin, Inc. to reprint "Moonlight Sonata" from *While Rome Burns* copyright 1934 by Alexander Woollcott, renewed © 1962 by Joseph Hennessey.

To Nancy Roberts to reprint "The Talking Corpse" from *Ghosts of the Carolinas*, copyright 1962 by Nancy Roberts and to reprint "The Crazy Quilt" from *South Carolina Ghosts from the Coast to the Mountains*, copyright 1983 by the University of South Carolina.

To Harold Matson Company, Inc., to reprint "The Partner" from *Book of the Eskimos*, copyright 1961 by Peter Freuchen.

To Dee Barber to reprint "The Mackenzie River Ghost" and "The Death of the Old Lion" from *Trail & Camp-fire Stories*, copyright 1940, 1944, 1947, 1950, 1965 by Julia M. Seton.

I also appreciate the editorial, typesetting, and proof reading help of Jane and Ruby Woodruff, Thomas A. Todd, and Keith Tutt.

From ghoulies and ghosties and long-leggety beasties
And things that go bump in the night, Good Lord, deliver us.

Cornish prayer

Table of Contents

Stories by Dr. Forgey, Ernest Thompson Seton, Peter Freuchen, Grey Owl, Mark Twain, Nancy Roberts, Alexander Woolcott, Augustus Hare, Ambrose Bierce, C. P. Cranch.

DO YOU WANT TO HEAR SOMETHING — REALLY SCARY?

This book was designed for the adult who needs a good, scary story to tell to youngsters in the 11 to 15 age group. Why scary stories? In 10 years of service as a scoutmaster to 3 different troops, and having worked with many other troops and groups of youngsters in summer camps and elsewhere, the most requested campfire event has been a good, scary story.

Humorous tales, Indian legends, parables, and educational stories all have their place. And indeed I have treated my scouts to all of them. But the most often verbalized request -- almost a challenge it seems -- is "scare me."

It might appear impossible to compete with the magnificent visual effects of videos and movies which particularly lend themselves to adventure stories. But actually a good story can have far greater entertainment impact. A story requires the listener to use his own imagination -- the movie spoon feeds its visual and sound effects, it leaves no room for personal imagination. No experience in the visual arts is more powerful than the human imagination.

Scary story telling is a craft and there are certain skills and techniques which should be utilized to be the most successful. Here are some aspects of this craft which should be employed for optimum results:

1. The storyteller must enjoy and have fun telling the story. Be relaxed. Do not be afraid of "hamming it up" a little, perhaps at times making a fool of oneself. Being stiff, formal, or even worried about the story will noticeably distract and make the listeners uncomfortable.

2. The storyteller should have eye to eye contact with the audience. This absolutely precludes reading a story. It must be memorized well enough that the story can be told without referring to notes or in any other way distracting from the intensity of the story at hand. I probably never tell the same story exactly the same twice. Get the general facts down and then improvise as necessary to keep the story moving smoothly.

3. Be in close physical contact with the audience. The closer the better. Being on a stage or behind a podium is terrible. Close contact is much easier to maintain in small groups than large ones. One has to make up for distance due to a large group with increased personal intensity and magnetism -- not always an easy order. Especially at first, keep the group small.

4. Do not get hung up on details -- yet it is details that can give a story its authenticity. Try not to get tripped up on names, dates, or other "facts" as children are quick to notice these discrepancies. There is certainly nothing wrong with making up these finishing touches as you go along. Each story in this book has an outline with details of names and other facts which can be changed by the storyteller. I will frequently use names to provide reality to a story at its beginning -- then if I have forgotten which name went with which character as the story unfolds, I simply work around this mental block calling the character by some other description (young man, old man, hunter, prospector, his friend, etc).

5. Set a quiet mood before beginning your story telling session. I find that tired audiences are best. Keep your group active during the day. The properly constructed evening program consumes extra energy and then quiets them down; it puts your listeners into a reflective and receptive mood. This is a must or the story telling should be put off to some other day. It is impolite to yourself or other members of the group to attempt telling a

story when some members are uncooperative or rowdy.

6. A campfire program is an ideal story telling medium. It is the perfect vehicle to use up that energy which young audiences have in such large quantities. As the campfire starts the program should include active participation parts with skits, songs, stunts -- all designed to include every audience member. Story telling by youngsters has to be limited as this can sometimes drag terribly, but a certain amount is fine. They can be involved in physically setting the program up and helping run it. Many fine books on organizing and running campfires, with suggestions for themes, can be found in the appendix. The end of the campfire, after the embers have burned down low, is the perfect time for telling a scary story.

7. While it is possible to have a story session, even a ''campfire program'' without a real campfire -- build one if it is at all possible. Who can help but feel a mystical sense of awareness when staring at the flames of a campfire? Frequently children are admonished not to play in a fire to prevent possible injury -- but who hasn't placed a stick in a fire, stirred the coals, and watched the swirling embers go skyward, pondering the mysteries of the universe? In a small group this can be allowed. In a bigger group generally a larger fire is built and the embers blaze skyward on their own. Regardless, a fire can play a very important part in setting the mood for a memorable story telling session.

8. It is totally unnecessary when telling an intense and scary story to use props, or to have a secret agent assist you by jumping out of the woods or dressing up in a strange fashion. In fact shenanigans of that nature distract from the basic story and take away from its credibility.

9. Use different inflections of voice to add moments of fear or excitement to your story. In general, tell a story with intensity and direct contact. At a certain point in the story where you know that the victim or person in the story might let out a scream -- break your intensity with a sudden shout or scream. With proper timing everyone listening will literally lift about two inches off their seats.

10. Really good scary stories need credibility. A ghost story

that has a detached hand crawling along the floor, trying to strangle its victims, might be entertaining, but it would not fulfill the request for a memorable scary story. If you start your story telling session with true or believable tales, the audience will be held in your grasp, spell bound.

Additional sources of campfire stories may by found in the books listed in the appendix. Frequently one may find good source material at libraries, in scary comic books, short story books, newspaper articles, folklore books, Indian stories, from inspiration at historical site markers, and in local legends. Books of short stories are frequently difficult to convert to campfire tales as the stories tend to be too long and contain too much important descriptive detail.

Each story in this book has been outlined to provide an easy refresher of plot and certain details for use prior to telling. The outline is in large type in case this book is being reviewed in the dim light of a flickering campfire.

Certain punctuations have been used in this book to aid in story telling. Words in CAPITAL LETTERS should be said loudly. Sentences ending with an exclamation mark (!) should be said rapidly, with great energy -- not loudly, but depending upon the circumstances with mystery or urgency. Phrases in capital letters with an exlamation mark mean to "let it all hang out." At times a phrase "AAAUUUGGGHHH" will appear. This is a loud shout or noise of some sort, the most comfortable loud vocal racket you can make. It does not have to be an "augh" sound -- just a good scary, sudden noise or scream.

Now, sit back, relax, and enjoy this book. Soon you will be able to say to your campers, "Do you want to hear something — REALLY scary?"

THE VALLEY OF
THE BLUE MIST

as told by Doc Forgey

About a hundred years ago there were three boys who decided that they would go to the gold fields in California and try to strike it rich. In those days, youngsters very often left home at an early age. The discovery of gold in California could mean wealth, perhaps more important, a chance for adventure and to leave hard and drab work in the East.

These three youngsters decided to band together -- after all, they had known each other all the way through grade school. They liked and trusted each other, and had helped one another often before. It was a dangerous long journey. They took the money that they had and were able to buy passage on an ocean going ship that would sail around Cape Horn off South America. They arrived in San Francisco and from there they headed to the gold fields.

Well, they were late in arriving. When the news of gold spreads, it spreads fast. Adventurers from all over the United States, from the Orient, from around the world had made the trek to California.

As they traveled to areas where the latest rumors told of great finds, they did so as part of a large, milling mob of eager gold seekers. Life was expensive. This was the frontier and everything had to be brought in from small communities that were not large enough to support such demands on their farms and craftsmen. Local farmers and workers had frequently deserted their work and had joined the gold seekers.

But a living COULD be scratched out, and who could tell, but anyone might strike it rich by finding a mother lode. So they joined the crowds and kept working the placer deposits, finding a little color (as gold was called when found mixed with the stream gravel). Placer deposits are hard work. Gold which has been washed down from the hills by the rivers is mixed with the stream gravel. By scooping up pans full of this mixture and washing the lighter stones away from the heavier gold, the prospectors could separate the valuable gold dust and nuggets.

But the goal was to find a Mother Lode -- the source of the placer gold. Prospectors always tried to follow the grains of gold up the river beds, hoping they would be led to the vein of gold from whence these nuggets were cut and carried by the water. Then, instead of washing and washing for mere specks of gold, they would have a solid vein of pure gold to cut away from the surrounding rock! They would have wealth beyond their wildest dreams!

One day the three boys came upon a river that only had a few miners working the placer deposits near a fairly large, but abandoned tent camp. They thought that there wouldn't be much gold there, otherwise there would be more miners. But when they started to pan, they found some of the best gold that they had come across! They were excited! By working this stream they could make a fortune if the gold held up!

Soon dusk approached. They joined the few other prospectors at the tent camp to cook supper and were invited to stay in an abandoned tent. They were amazed at how rich this stream was, and yet how few miners were working there.

An old man told them, "You need not be surprised boys. You may not be here long either. There are things more important than gold! But whatever you do as long as you stay in this valley, get into the tents by night-fall. Don't get caught in the valley in the blue mist. People die who get caught by it. It carries some sickness, but we have survived it. Do as we do, get into your tent before the blue mist comes down the valley!''

And that night, the blue mist again came. At first fingers of a thick blue fog rolled down the valley and curled around the tents. It was dark, about 10:00 p.m., and the lantern cast an eerie glow with the fog lapping higher and higher on the tents, until finally all was obscured.

The three friends were safe in a tent, hardly believing what the old timers had told them, but not wishing to dare their luck either. Day after day they worked the riches of this stream; night after night they sought refuge in the tents as the blue mist slid down the river from higher in the valley, obscuring everything and bringing all activity outside the camp to a stop.

And as they would work any other river, by day they panned further and further upstream, looking for richer color, looking for a concentration of gold that might mean that they were nearing the Mother Lode. But they always made sure to heed the old mens' advice to be back in the tent camp by night-fall, long before the fingers of blue mist curled down the valley.

One day they spotted an abandoned cabin, high in the valley. Its door was unlocked and upon checking it out they found it fully furnished, apparently abandoned by the owner. That night they asked the old timers about this cabin, so conveniently located high in the valley closer to the richer source of placer deposits which they had worked their way to.

''Stay in the cabin by day, if you must. But whatever you do, get back to this camp by night fall. Don't let your greed cause you to get caught out there over night. That cabin wasn't abandoned -- the owner was Bill Murphy, who some say was the first prospector in this valley. He died in that cabin, and by the way they found him it was a horrible death. The same horrible death that kills anyone caught by the blue mist.''

More than that the old timers couldn't tell them. But they were obviously afraid for their lives. The valley and its blue mist was holding some terrible secret and these old men would be of no help in solving the mystery.......

Mike, one of the three boys, finally had enough of the long trek back down to the tent camp, especially when there was a

fully equipped cabin so close to their diggings. He announced
one day that he was spending the night in the cabin. That morning
he took his bedding, several days of his rations, and packed them
along to the diggings. Tom and Roy tried to talk him out of it.

"Why take the chance?" Tom asked. "We have it OK at
the tent camp. We are making good money. And it's obvious
something terrible has happened in this valley. Those old miners
aren't afraid of anything, except the blue mist. Let's just stay
together and forget that cabin!"

Mike wouldn't hear of it. He worked with them during the
day, but that night Tom and Roy had to return to the tent camp
without him. And as the night wore on, they anxiously awaited
the coming of the mist.

About 10:00 p.m., as usual, the fingers of thick, blue mist
curled through the tent camp -- soon obscuring all view of the
twinkling light from the cabin up the valley. Finally, about 1:00
a.m., they heard something -- they thought -- way up the valley,
possibly from the cabin. Tom couldn't believe that they had let
Mike stay up there alone.

"We promised each other that we would stick together, no
matter what," he reminded Roy. The old prospectors were furious
that they had let Mike stay up there, for they had learned to like
these three boys from the East. They didn't want anything to
happen to them, and here they had gone and challenged the
deadly blue mist.

The night was terribly long. Tom and Roy couldn't sleep
that night as they waited for dawn so they could scramble up the
valley to the cabin. The old prospectors also spent the night
awake, worrying about their new friend.

But morning finally did come and they left as soon as the
sun shined into the valley over the mountains, burning off the
blue mist and sending light into the dark valley.

When they got to the cabin, they couldn't believe their eyes!
Mike was dead. And worse, the cabin door was open and he lay
half out of the door with a look of terror frozen on his face. A
fear that struck the others right to the heart. The old men said
that they had enough, they were leaving this valley for help. It

wasn't safe to stay any longer, no matter how much gold was there.

Roy and Tom were stunned! And sick at their loss. And mad that they had not helped their friend as they had promised when they set out from home together.

In a daze they returned to the now abandoned tent camp after burying their friend near the cabin. They had to decide what to do. Should they return home to tell Mike's parents? They had enough money to return home, but not enough to buy a farm or to start a business if they returned now to the East. But more than that, they mourned their friend. This mourning turned to anger and frustration. Tom finally told Roy that they could not leave until they had done something to solve the mystery of their friend's death. They could not go home without being able to tell Mike's parents what had actually happened. Some beast or some person must be responsible for this, and whoever -- or whatever -- it must be punished.

Tom could think of only one way to do this. They must return to the cabin, armed, and spend the night. That way they could solve the mystery of the Valley of the Blue Mist!

Roy was horrified! No way was he going to spend the night in that cabin! He thought the idea was crazy and he told Tom so in no uncertain terms. Tom was rigid in his plan. He felt that it was their duty as they had abandoned their friend -- they owed this to him.

Roy could not talk him out of it. But there was no way that HE would go up that valley and spend the night in the blue mist. As evening approached, the boys each had their mind made up. Tom packed his gear, including their only rifle, and headed up the valley to the cabin. It was already late when he left, and he had to hurry to beat the blue mist.

When he got there he made sure that the door was latched and windows shut. He moved the heavy table in front of the door, and to help support it, also slid the heavy chest of drawers against it.

Down in the valley Roy was alone in the tent camp. The old timers had left in a hurry, not even taking their equipment.

An old clock ticked on as night fell. He realized what a terrible error he had made. His friend was trapped at the cabin, he was alone in this dreadful valley. Just two nights ago he had been with the two best friends he ever had -- without a care in the world. Now he was exhausted, alone without a rifle, and his remaining friend was at the head of a valley that was full of death and mystery.

The minutes on the old wind up clock ticked by. A proud possession of one of the miners, it had been left behind in the hasty abandonment of the camp. Soon it was 10:00 p.m.; the fingers of mist again curled through the silent tent camp. Terror struck -- he waited and listened. He could hear nothing. The swirling mist climbed higher and soon obscured all view of the stars and the other tents. He was utterly alone. Oh, how he wished he had stuck with Tom in the cabin -- or wherever he wanted to go. After all, Tom was his best friend and might even now be needing his help. And how about him -- alone and without a gun in abandoned tents -- alone in a thick, swirling mist.

The night lasted and lasted, as nights full of terror always do. Soon the glow of the sun penetrated the thick fog, and the mist started lifting from the valley.

Roy scrambled up the valley to the cabin. From the river's edge he shouted for Tom -- but there was no answer from the cabin! He climbed up the path ...

AAAUUUGGGHHH!

THERE AT THE FRONT OF THE CABIN -- THE DOOR OPENED, WAS HIS FRIEND'S BODY! Twisted in an agony of death, the table and dresser knocked over, the rifle off to one side. The rifle had not even been fired! What could possibly have caught brave Tom so suddenly that he couldn't even get a shot off?

Roy now knew what he had to do. He could not return home now, he had to find out what mystery the Blue Mist held. He had to avenge his friends' deaths! Oh, how he wished he had stayed with Tom. How could he have been so stupid to have let him stay in this cabin alone, but now he had to make all of that up to both of his friends.

He immediately returned to the tent camp. There he got nails and a hammer. He brought extra kerosene for the lantern and two extra lanterns. He brought rope and some old, empty cans. He would return to that cabin and avenge the death of his friends, come what may!

Weighted down with his supplies, he took a last look at the now abandoned tent camp. He trudged up the now familiar stream bed that he and his friends had worked together for so long.

At the cabin he noted that the old clock which his friends had started was still ticking, and the time seemed correct. He took nails and went to work on the windows, boarding them up -- nailing them soundly shut. Nothing could possibly get in. He strung the empty cans on the rope around the cabin, so he could hear anyone, or anything, approach. He raked the dirt so that he could see any foot prints the next day. Finally, everything outside seemed ready. He shut the door of the cabin for the last time, and firmly nailed it shut.

He moved the dresser in front of the door. Thinking to further barricade it, he tried to move the large trunk located along one wall of the cabin. The trunk was incredibly heavy, too heavy to move. Opening it he found only a layer of old clothes, a belt, and a few odd items. The trunk had been nailed to the floor. Leaving it there, he filled the kerosene lanterns. He made sure the rifle was loaded, and then started the long wait for night.

Night comes suddenly in the mountains. When the sun finally lowers towards the horizon, it will suddenly dip behind a mountain top and be quickly lost from view. Shadows appear immediately and soon thereafter it is night.

With night in this valley comes more than darkness. The dreaded blue mist starts forming in the chasms and rivulets that form the valley on the mountain side. As Roy waited, he watched the clock. Soon it was 10:00 p.m., and the mist started swirling beyond the cabin door, filling the basin of the river and sliding its way down to the abandoned tent camp. Fingers of mist slid between now empty tents.

At the cabin Roy continued to wait. His heart pounding, he thought of his friends and he thought of his own danger. The night deepened and outside the mist covered the cabin. He listened intently for any sound amongst the tin cans outside, any evidence of movement from the nearby forest.

And finally he DID hear something. At first it was a quiet whisper. Then, more of a hiss. It sounded close, very close to the cabin. Could it be a snake? Or a whole coil of snakes? Surely there would have been some sign earlier when the others had been killed.

The hiss was close, near the window. SUDDENLY HE FELT A TIGHT CONSTRICTION GRABBING AT HIS THROAT. He thought he was losing his sight, the cabin was becoming darker! No! It was the kerosene lights, they were flickering out!

AAAUUUGGGHHH!

VIOLENT SPASMS TWITCHED HIS BODY, HE GASPED FOR AIR, HE STRUGGLED TO ESCAPE! He couldn't breathe! The light from the lamps was out, the hissing, more of a sighing was louder now. Its location was easy to identify -- IT WAS COMING FROM THE EMPTY TRUNK!

He grabbed at the dresser and threw it aside. The planks! He ripped at the planks, the spasm racking his body!

Early the next day a column of men proceeded up the valley. It was the group of old miners, leading a posse from the nearest town. Upon finding the cabin sealed shut, they took their pikes to the door and smashed their way through. Inside they found the contorted body of the last of the three friends.

These men decided that they would take matters into their own hands. Furiously they would destroy this cabin where so many had died. They started tearing it apart, board by board. When they reached the flooring, they too noted the old trunk nailed to the floor. Breaking it apart they made an incredible discovery. The trunk apparently had a secret, false bottom. It covered a shaft leading into a hidden mine. And that mine proved to be the Mother Lode! Rather than claiming this rich vein of ore for what it was, the miner had simply staked a claim and built his cabin over the spot. Then he concealed the shaft opening with the trunk, a much better concealment than a trap door under a rug in the cabin. But unknown to the old miner, he eventually reached a pocket of deadly gas within his mine. When night fell in the valley, the barometric pressure dropped. On the outside this caused the blue mist to rise up from the ground. But inside the cabin, it allowed the mine shaft to start blowing air out its opening, just as a cave entrance will do when the pressure is right. But this mine air was laced with deadly cyanide gas, which, when it caught its victim, racked them with spasm and a very quick death.

This mine eventually became known as the Empress Mine, one of the richest finds of the gold fields. But a mine with a tragic beginning, one that killed three good friends in the midst of their life of adventure together.

STORY OUTLINE

I. Three young friends left their homes in the East, about a hundred years ago, to try their luck in the western gold rush.

II. They were panning for gold, like most prospectors -- but always hoping they could follow the gold specks to the Mother Lode, the vein of pure gold from whence the rivers washed the nuggets.

III. They found a beautiful valley with only a few prospectors. Much to their surprise the panning was rich in gold yield. An old miner told them of the legend of the valley -- he warned them to be inside camp before the dreaded blue mist formed in the valley at night. Some people die when caught out in the blue mist.

IV. The boys worked further and further upstream,

panning a higher and higher yield of gold. The distance to camp was becoming longer each night. Finally they found a cabin which had been abandoned way up the valley.

V. Mike, one of the boys, decided to spend his nights there, rather than make the long trek back to camp. The others couldn't talk him out of it.

VI. Tom and Roy couldn't sleep that night worrying about their friend. Finally daylight came and the mist burned off. When they and the other prospectors reached the cabin they found Mike dead, half lying out of the cabin, with a look of terror frozen on his face.

VII. The miners left for help, but Tom and Roy stayed behind. Tom told Roy that they had to find out what had killed their friend. He insisted on spending the night in the cabin with the rifle. Roy could not talk him out of it, but there was no way that he would spend the night out in the valley of the blue mist.

VIII. That night Tom barricaded himself into the cabin, moving the heavy furniture that was there and spent the night, his rifle ready for any trouble.

IX. Roy was alone in the tent camp, afraid for himself and his friend. The next morning he scrambled up the valley to the cabin and there AAAUUUGGGHHH! (loud scream) was his friend's body, twisted in an agony of death, the door open, the rifle off to one side, unused.

X. Roy was now determined to avenge his two friends' deaths. He gathered supplies at the cabin, returned to it and nailed the door shut, covered the windows, and sat waiting for the mystery of the valley of the blue mist.

XI. Finally, in the night he heard a hiss that grew louder and louder. He realized that the hiss was coming from the trunk that was nailed to the floor of the cabin. Suddenly he started choking, gasping for air.

XII. The prospectors returned the next day with a posse from the nearest town. They found Roy's body and decided to tear the cabin down. When doing this they found that the trunk was covering a mine shaft entrance. It was the entrance to the Mother Lode.

XIII. But the mine had encountered deadly poisonous cyanide gas -- and when the night came and the barometric pressure dropped, when the blue mist formed outside, at that time the mine entrance would start blowing air out, rather than sucking it in. And the poison gas would claim another victim.

XIV. The mine became famous as the Empress Mine, one of the richest ever discovered. But a mine that killed its discoverer and three good friends in the midst of their life of adventure together.

THE HUMAN HAND

as told by Doc Forgey

Introduction

Stories to be good have to be credible. An example I gave earlier was the ridiculous situation of a severed human hand crawling along the ground trying to strangle its victims. The following is a story utilizing a human hand, but told in a manner that lends it credibility. I have been told that this is actually a true story. It is a story that has circulated about my old alma mater, Indiana University, and it is supposed to have happened back in the 1930s.

* * * * *

The girls in a particular sorority at Indiana University, back in the 1930's, had a terrible thing happen to them.[1] A group of six of them were being dated by a particular group of boys. This group had become very close. They shared all of their free time together and generally enjoyed talking about all of the things which they did during the day. Whenever you are in school,

---

[1] If telling this story to a group of young scouts, you may have to tell them what a sorority is.

working, or doing anything during the day -- what do you talk about when you get together at night? Well, generally it's about what happened during the day. You talk about the professors you have, the tests they gave, your other classmates -- even though you are trying to get away from it and want to relax at night. You know yourselves, you frequently talk about what you did during the day. And the same was true of this group.

There was a law student, two business students, a chemistry major, and also two pre-medical students. And therein laid the problem. Because one of the girls was extremely squeamish. She couldn't stand hearing them tell stories about the laboratories, about cutting up cadavers (human bodies), about doing any of their work. So these two poor kids could never say anything about what they were doing during the day. At first this was OK, but as time went on it became a real nuisance to everyone concerned -- all of the others felt kind of sorry that this situation was going on. But she was just absolutely rigid about it -- she would not let them discuss the things that they did in class.

One day they all got together talking, when she wasn't with them, and they thought: "You know, we ought to teach her a lesson. We ought to do something to just kind of get rid of this nonsense." And they came up with an idea...

Now in Indiana during the winter it gets dark rather early, around 4:30 p.m. They decided they would tell her that they wanted to go out for a movie after supper. It would be very dark.

In this sorority all of the girls had their rooms upstairs, but they ate their meals and entertained their guests in their living rooms and dining room on the first floor. In their individual rooms upstairs the girls had electric lights, but because it was so many years ago, the fixtures were very simple. Every light was simply turned on by pulling a string that hung down from the ceiling.

The plan was that they would go to the cadaver laboratory where they kept the dead bodies. There they would cut off a human hand. And they would take that human hand and they would tie it to the electric light switch string hanging from her ceiling. They would make an excuse so that she would have to go up to that room alone. And when she went up to that room, she would reach up to turn on the light, and she would GRAB THAT HUMAN HAND!

So, sure enough, the boys arranged it. They managed to sneak a hand out of the cadaver laboratory. That night they all sat around and had supper together over at the sorority before going to a movie. It soon got dark out. Finally they were sitting around discussing their evening, when one of the boys said "Isn't it about time that we left for the movies? And the girls all said "Oh, yes. Let's get our coats." And they all stood up as if they were about to rush on upstairs, but then the five of them knowing this trick that they were about to play -- and which had already been arranged by one of the boys during supper -- hung back seemingly to make last minute minor conversations with their boy friends, while she went up stairs ... to turn on that light!

And as she disappeared around the corner of the stairs, they all fell silent. They were waiting for the scream.

A scream that never came.

Finally, they could not stand the suspense any longer. They all as a group traveled up the stairs, not caring that boys were not allowed upstairs, and they looked down the hall of the dorm.

Nobody ... nothing was in sight.

The door was standing open to her room ... and the light was on!

They rushed down the hall and they OPENED THE DOOR TO THAT ROOM -- nobody was there.

One of the girls went down to the end of the hall to the bathroom, opened the door, went in ... nothing. She wasn't there.

ALL OF A SUDDEN ONE OF THE BOYS RAISED THE SKIRT AROUND THE BOTTOM OF THE BED ... nothing was under the bed.

They couldn't believe it. The light was on, the hand was gone, the room was empty. Where was she?

Then one of them went over to the closet door.. OPENED UP THE CLOSET DOOR -- AND THERE SHE WAS! DOWN AT THE BOTTOM OF THAT CLOSET! HER HAIR TURNED

SOLID WHITE... AND SHE WAS GNAWING ON THAT HUMAN HAND.

She had gone entirely insane. She had grabbed that hand off the string and just started gnawing on it. She was totally mad. They had to take her away from school and she had to be locked up the rest of her life in an insane asylum. The boys were afraid that they might be kicked out of school, so they took that gnawed human hand from her and drove it outside of town and buried it. They buried it in a place that to this very day can be found on the maps -- a little town just east of Bloomington called "Gnaw Bone, Indiana!"

STORY OUTLINE

I. A group of 6 boys were dating girls from a sorority at Indiana University back in the 1930s.

II. While they all liked to talk about their actions during the day, one of the girls was so squeamish that she would not let the two boys who were medical students talk about any of their activities.

III. The group finally decided to pull a trick on her to cure her squeamish ways. The medical students stole a hand from a dead body and hung it from the light string in her room.

IV. After supper, during a dark winter evening, the girl went upstairs to get her coat before going to a movie.

V. They waited to hear her scream, but no scream ever came.

VI. They scooted upstairs, but could find no sign of her in the room, down the hall, or under the bed.

VII. Finally, they looked in the closet and there they found her ... totally insane, gnawing, eating on that human hand!

THE STORY OF
LA CUCARACHA MINE

as told by Doc Forgey

No so many years ago there was a group of young men, a little older than you boys, who were in college. They developed a hobby, and that hobby was to try and find buried treasure. They felt that the best way of doing that was to learn Spanish. Not regular Spanish, but the old Spanish, the Spanish spoken by the *conquistadores*. These ancient soldiers had captured the Indians of Central America -- the Inca, the Mayan, the Aztec. Stealing their gold and other treasures, they would bring it back to Spain in their galleons. They kept meticulous records because this gold was the property of the king. The instant they laid their hands on it, it was considered the king's property. So they kept very good track of it -- their lives were forfeit were they to lose their accounting of these treasures.

In Spain at the Alhambra, the old royal castle where these records were sent, there are piles of ancient documents which are old records of the gold shipments. The boys felt that within those archives there could be some secret that might let them find a lost treasure. Indeed they studied these records carefully. They went over there during the summer and spent weeks and weeks poring over all sorts of these ancient journals. They had explained to the officials that they were there for academic purposes and therefore they were allowed access to the archives to help their studies.

One summer they found it. There was a record of a mine, a very rich mine, located in a province that today is in southern Mexico. The Spaniards were running it with Indian slave labor and getting tremendous quantities of gold. Year after year the gold was being shipped back to Spain, when suddenly ... it stopped!

Something mysterious had happened. There was no more gold from this area.

Several things could have happened. The Indians could have mutinied and actually killed off the guards. But if that were to have happened, the Spaniards would have sent more guards and an army detail to restore order, for this was a very wealthy mine. So that could not have been it. A disease could have struck killing off everyone in that area. But again, with that much value to this mine, surely the mine would have been reopened regardless of the cost.

Something mysterious had happened to have caused this whole operation to have just closed down. The name given to the mine was: *"La Cucaracha"*.

The three young friends took all of the money that they had and formed an expedition to go down deep into the jungles of lower Mexico. They had an approximate location from the old Spanish name of the district, and so they went to find *La Cucaracha*.

They went to small towns in the highlands on the jungle edge to see if they could get any clue about where some mysterious things may have occurred. In one town there was a bar with an old man there -- he did not know anything about *La Cucaracha*, but he said: "You know, there is an Indian legend about a mine called: *La Antigua*, in the back country. It means "The Old One."

That was the closest of anything they had come upon, the only thing that they had to go with, it certainly sounded mysterious. Maybe the Indians had a different name for the mine than the Spanish Conquistadores. They asked the old man to take them to *La Antigua* and they headed off into the jungles on their quest.

They cut their way through the thick underbrush, SLASH-ING their way through the foliage, and finally after they had gotten way out in the jungles they found a mysterious shaft. This shaft HAD to be man made. It was cut out of solid rock, a shaft that just disappeared into the depths of the bedrock of the earth.

They had to find out what was at the bottom of this pit. They dropped a rock down it ... they could hear nothing. So they rigged up a wench, and one of the guys climbed into a parachute harness. The Indians working with his two friends would lower him into the shaft.

He had a head light on. Soon he was below the surface of the ground and the darkness of the musty pit closed in around him. As he was being lowered further and further into the shaft, the rope started to slowly spin around. He slowly twirled around and around as he went down deeper and deeper. Pretty soon he could see no light from the top of the shaft at all. There was just a tiny light way up above as he was being lowered into that shaft.

As he was being lowered deeper and deeper, he noticed that the walls were turning a rusty brown color. As he went further down he thought that maybe he could see the bottom of this mine shaft. But he was spinning faster and faster, too fast to clearly make out what was below.

He needed to slow down, so he reached his leg way out to touch the wall of the mine shaft to stop the rapid spinning. As he did this, while spinning around, his foot literally gouged into the wall of the shaft -- suddenly he realized what that rust color was. Thousands, millions of cockroaches had climbed up the side of the shaft -- indeed as he looked further down he could see that the bottom of the shaft -- the place to which he was being lowered -- was a teeming mass of cockroaches. He was being lowered to his death, he was about to be buried alive by cockroaches!

AAAUUUGGGHHH! He shouted as loud as he could, hoping his friends would hear him and stop lowering him into that ocean of writhing insects.

His foot had dislodged the cockroaches on the walls and millions came cascading down, some falling, thousands flying.

A suffocating mass of whirling wings. Trying to get his breath for a second scream he choked on a mouth full of the vile insects. They were in his ears, in his nose, his throat gagged with wriggling, struggling insects. He was suffocating, he was gagging -- trying to scream and vomit at the same time.

He had learned the dread secret of *La Cucaracha* Mine.

And closer to the bottom of this pit -- closer to being buried alive in a mountain of cockroaches. All light from his helmet obscured by the massive number of insects, he knew he was closer and closer to the bottom of the shaft. THOUSANDS, AND THOUSANDS OF THE ROACHES POUNDED HIM ON ALL SIDES. HE COULDN'T GET HIS BREATH, BUT HE HAD TO BREATHE! Desperately he struggled for air.

They were down his shirt, swarming around his head, thousands, and thousands of them.

HELP!!!! His screams were muffled by the millions of whirling cockroaches. He shouted again, and he shouted again -- desperate for help amongst this nightmare of cockroaches. Cascading cockroaches were burying him alive!

Suddenly ... he jerked to a stop!

He felt himself being raised, raised as rapidly as he knew his friends could. Once on the surface, he lay gagging and choking -- trying to breath. His friends on the surface realized something was wrong. Thousands of cockroaches suddenly began swarming out of the entrance to the shaft, and when they saw that they stopped lowering him and immediately tried to get their friend out of there. They now all knew the secret of *La Cucaracha*!

Subsequently the village people made certain that the shaft was boarded up so that never again would somebody be lowered into the sprawling mass of insects that had taken over *La Cucaracha* mine.

STORY OUTLINE

I. A group of students study old spanish documents to study the movement of the gold taken from the New World by the conquistadores.

II. They learn of a mine called *La Cucaracha* whose rich supply of gold suddenly and mysteriously stopped.

III. Forming an expedition to the section of Mexico where the mine should be located, they find a deep shaft in the jungle.

IV. One of the young men is lowered into the pit. As the rope starts spinning faster and faster, he notices that the walls of the shaft are turning a rusty brown color.

V. He thinks that he might be able to see the bottom of the shaft. Putting out his foot, he touches the wall to stop his spin. Suddenly, he dislodges a mass of cockroaches.

VI. He tries to shout to his friends to stop lowering him into the pit of cockroaches, but the flying insects practically suffocate him, preventing his friends from hearing him.

VII. Just as he is about to be lowered to his death, his friends stop lowering him. They have been alerted to his trouble by the flying hoards of cockroaches that start coming out of the shaft entrance.

VIII. They have learned the secret of *La Cucaracha* -- the Cockroach Mine.

THE PARTNER

as told by Peter Freuchen [1]

Introduction

Peter Freuchen's first visit to the land of the Eskimos was in 1906 when he went on the Danish Expedition to Greenland. In 1910, along with Knud Rasmussen, he founded a trading station which he named Thule. Until his death in Alaska in 1957 he spent every moment he could in the northern Arctic regions, living with the trappers, traders, and natives of this vast area.

The following is a true tale of the north country, one of the best campfire stories that I have ever read.

* * * * *

IT'S OFTEN HARD TO TELL what makes a man go up to the Arctic year after year, until he has spent maybe half a lifetime in the Polar regions. Sometimes it is a tradition in a family. Boys follow in the footsteps of their fathers and become experienced trappers before they are out of their teens. Their lot is nothing to envy. The profit is small and most of these sturdy

---

[1] Reprinted by permission of Harold Matson Company, Inc., from *Book of the Eskimos*, copyright 1961 by Peter Freuchen.

men could make a better living at home or as sailors going south to a comfortable life instead of north to the arctic darkness. But there is something which pulls these men northward, something which never lets go of a man once he has been up there a year or two.

There are those, of course, who are not suited for the loneliness in the Arctic. They have to get out at once. And there are some who are disappointed when they find arctic life is not an uninterrupted series of adventures. There is, naturally, much in the life of an arctic trapper which is different from anything at home, but his Polar existence is essentially monotonous. The Arctic is always the same: cold, dark and indifferent.

Most of the trappers and sailors I have known in the Arctic are no different from other people; they are solid and normal men. They can take the loneliness, but the darkness is sometimes too much of a strain on the nerves. When a man is left utterly alone for four months of darkness, an event that interrupts his known routine often presents a situation he cannot master.

I remember a man like that, whose nerves snapped under the strain. He was a good trapper and a fine fellow who had spent winter after winter in Greenland. His name was Olav, and since he is still alive, I shall not mention his last name. He was an old-timer in Greenland. A simple man, perhaps, without much learning or imagination, but as good as they come and a first-rate trapper. I had known him for many years, and he had always spent the winter in Greenland with the same partner, Thomas Vold. The two of them went up and stayed alone together, miles and miles from the nearest man, until they were picked up in spring to go south with their catch. But one year Olav quarreled with Thomas about his share in the catch, with the inevitable result that the partnership split up. The next year Olav got himself a new partner.

I was serving then as first mate on the Blue Whale, the ship which brought the trappers up to Greenland. As soon as Olav came aboard with all his supplies, he introduced me to the new man. His name was Gustav Krakau, and I knew right away that he was a stranger to Greenland. Gustav Krakau, Olav told me

later, had never before been out of Denmark. He had some
money, apparently, and he had paid more than his share of the
supplies. That may have been part of the reason why Olav let
himself be talked into taking along such an inexperienced man,
but I think it was just as much due to Gustav Krakau's manner
and the way he talked. Even the old-timers seemed to like him
and trust him.

They had quite a lot of supplies along, more than we were
used to, and we teased Olav about it. The old man is a millionaire
now, the boys said, look at all the stuff he has along; crates and
crates of dried fruits and cans and cans of fancy stuff. We got
it all on board and left the next morning, but the first day out
Gustav Krakau got sick as a dog. Nobody made anything of it
at first, but Olav did not like it. He felt it was a reflection on
his own reputation to have his partner behave as a landlubber,
and that made it all the worse. The crew began pulling his leg,
joking day and night about "the tough new partner." Krakau
stayed in his bunk and didn't touch any food, but as soon as we
were in the ice and the sea got calm, he was all right again.
Once he came on deck and we got to talk to him, he turned out
to be a man who knew a little bit about everything. He didn't
talk much about himself, but he seemed to come from a good
family. He had brought along a lot of books to read during the
winter, something unusual for a trapper.

Olav was in for teasing again, about the Greenland library.
He wasn't very proud of all the books, but he stood up for his
partner, declaring that there was no law against a trapper reading
if he felt like it.

After a few days, we came to the fjord where Olav had had
his blockhouse for many years. The two men left us with all
their boxes and crates and stood waving good-by to us as we
sailed out of the fjord and turned north again.

When the Blue Whale came back for them next summer,
Olav was alone. As soon as we approached the bottom of the
fjord, we could see that something was wrong. When Thomas
Vold was Olav's partner, the two of them always came out in
the rowboat to meet the Blue Whale, as all the trappers do unless

they have lost the boat during the winter.

No boat came out to meet us. We could see the dogs running around on shore, but at first there was not a soul to be seen. At last Olav came out of the blockhouse, alone. He was a ghastly sight. He looked like a broken man.

He just stood there waiting for us and as soon as I came on shore, I noticed in a little patch of clear ground behind the blockhouse a simple wooden cross. A name had been carefully carved in the wood -- Gustav Krakau -- with the date of death.

We could hardly get a word of explanation from Olav. He had the looks of a haunted man; his eyes were shifty, and he looked away when we talked to him.

Finally, the skipper decided to open the grave. Olav refused to go with us. He did not want to come near that little wooden cross. We got out some spades and soon the body was uncovered. Gustav Krakau had a large hole in his head. It didn't take much knowledge to see that he had been shot; a great part of his head had been blown off. And still we didn't know just what had happened. It might have been an accident, but Olav would not explain. We would have to report the death as soon as we got back, of course, and we had to bring Olav with us to the proper authorities. The skipper told me to put together some kind of coffin for the body of Gustav Krakau and we set off again.

The return trip was a miserable affair for Olav and the rest of us. He walked around by himself, never talking to us, just looking at us with his scared, restless eyes. Most of the time he spent alone in his cabin, muttering to himself, never turning up for any meals.

As soon as we reached port, the passengers went on shore and nobody stopped Olav from leaving with them. But the skipper went straight to the authorities to give his report, and the following day Olav was arrested.

I think it was only after they put him in prison that Olav finally went out of his mind. I think I can swear to it that he was still normal on the trip home, but he had felt all our eyes on him -- questioning, curious, accusing.

I was present in the sheriff's office when Olav made his

statement the following day and told the whole weird tale of that winter. He was hesitant at first, incoherent and confused, but once he really got going, nobody could stop him. His worn hands were twisting nervously and his eyes looking off in the distance as he began:

"I should never have taken him along, of course. I can see it now, but that's only because one knows so much afterwards. I can see it as I sit here and I'll try to tell you all about it because I want you, I want somebody to understand what really happened. You may still not understand it, Sheriff, but perhaps it doesn't matter too much."

And without holding anything back, hesitating only now and then to fumble for the right word, this shadow of the Olav we had known gave his account of Gustav Krakau's first and last winter in Greenland. He began right at the beginning, the moment when the Blue Whale left them in the little fjord.

Gustav had been very eager and excited, but that first moment when they were left alone, he had suddenly grown solemn. He grabbed Olav's hand and promised to show himself worthy of all the confidence and friendship the older man had shown him. Olav didn't care for such talk. He told Gustav gruffly that it was all nonsense, turned his back on him, and told him to carry up their gear to the blockhouse as fast as he could.

After the first few days with Gustav Krakau, Olav knew he had never met a better man for a companion. Gustav was clever and he learned fast. He had never seen a walrus before, but as soon as he was shown how to hit the animal right behind the ear, he got the knack of it in no time. He had no idea about skinning and flensing animals, but he stood watching Olav like a little boy. Then he asked for permission to do the next walrus himself, in order to learn it. And he worked all night long before he was satisfied.

He was a wizard in the kitchen. Olav had never seen cooking like it. Besides the usual supplies, Gustav had brought along all sorts of things: curry and spice sauces and stuff Olav had never heard about. The way he made the food made Olav feel like staying on at table long after the meal was finished, just to keep the good taste in his mouth.

From the time he was a small boy, Gustav had done a good deal of hunting in the woods at home. He had dreamed of being a trapper one day, but his mother had kept him from it. She wanted him to study, that was why he had plowed through so many books. It got to be a habit with him, and he kept on reading.

He was a good man with a gun, and he and Olav had plenty of meat during the late summer. When fall came with the first frost, they saw their first bear. Gustav got all excited and asked if he might have the first shot. Olav told Gustav to go ahead. Gustav was like a child when he felled the bear, and he made a real good job of it. Later on, they saw bears every day, several big ones in one day sometimes. Gustav skinned them all and he studied their insides to see what they had been eating. He did the same with all the animals, and he wrote down in his books what he saw.

After a while, it was getting noticeably darker every day, and soon the sun would be gone for a good many months. It was time to set the traps, and that was something new to Gustav. He worked at it at home by the blockhouse first, and he got to be pretty good at it. In no time he caught on to the trick of setting the traps and covering them with a thin layer of snow to hide them from the fox. In a couple of days he was as good as Olav, and they set out together. At first Olav went with him, showing him where to put the traps and how to find them again when he came back.

After that, the two men split up the territory between them. Everything to the north was Gustav's, while Olav kept to the south. They made a regular routine out of it. Every Monday morning they set out with two dogs each. The dogs pulled the little sleighs with the sleeping bags and food and they could move faster that way. Olav had had the same four dogs for years, and it was funny the way they took to Gustav right away. The old partner, Thomas Vold, had always had a hard time getting along with them, but Gustav had a wonderful way with the animals and they were friends from the first day.

Gustav went north and Olav south and they kept walking

away from each other all day Monday and Tuesday. At night, they slept in some small huts which Olav had built years before. Half of Wednesday they kept on walking, checking the traps, but in the afternoon they turned around. Wednesday they slept in the Tuesday huts and Thursday night they spent in the Monday huts. Friday they were back at the blockhouse again. If they met a snowstorm, they had to stay over in one of the small huts, of course, and they wouldn't get back until Saturday. Sometimes they did not meet again until Sunday, and once in a long while they did not see each other until the end of the next week again. But Olav had stored plenty of food in all the huts, they were both careful, and he knew he did not have to worry about Gustav.

Soon he noticed that he was really looking forward to Friday. He began missing Gustav when he was all alone with the dogs, and he was eager to sit listening to his strange partner again. Life with Gustav was quite different from all the winters he had spent with Thomas Vold. They hardly spoke a word to each other, Olav and Thomas. What did they have to talk about? They knew the work and did it well enough, both of them. That was all. Gustav was the opposite. He always had lots to tell when they met again. During the week he had seen so many things he had to talk about -- things Olav and Thomas always had known but never talked about, because they did not seem worth wasting a word on.

What a talker Gustav was! When Olav was alone again during the week, he couldn't help thinking of all the things Gustav had said. In the end he got so used to all this talk that be began saying things on his own.

After a while, it got to be with Gustav just like with the heat in a house: you can do without it, but you get mighty cold. Olav missed him more and more during the week; Gustav made the winter quite different for him.

Christmas came and they had something extra to eat, they even washed and shaved themselves and lit candles. Olav put on a clean white shirt. After all, he thought, it's Christmas only once a year. But Gustav did not seem to be moved by the Holy Day. He went out to check his traps just like any other day. Olav didn't like it, but there was nothing he could do, since they were partners and Gustav was just as good a trapper by then as he was himself.

It was shortly after New Year's Day when Gustav complained that he didn't feel so well. His arms and legs were like lead if he walked any distance. Olav could see that he moved very slowly and went early to bed, but he always took a book along with him and told Olav about some of the things he read. Olav never understood much of what was read to him, but he listened carefully and thought about it afterward.

The next Monday they got ready as usual. Gustav still moved slowly, but he seemed all right as they parted. They said good-by to each other and trotted off again, one to the north and the other to the south. The week went by like any other, Olav looked after his traps and had a pretty good load with him when he returned on Friday. Gustav's dogs were by the blockhouse already, and Olav could see the lights in the house. It was the first time Gustav had returned before him, but when Olav entered, he found the other man in bed, looking very sick. Gustav told him he had had some fever and had returned the day after they parted. He had felt pretty bad for a while, but he was all right again, he said. He had only wanted to wait for Olav before he set out to make up for the time he had lost. Now he wanted to leave right away to get the animals in his traps before the wolves got them.

He was right, of course. They had to think of the catch before anything else; that was what they were there for. Olav didn't say anything, although he had been looking forward to spending the weekend with Gustav. He felt very lonely as his partner left. He had never thought of it before, but now he knew that Gustav had spoiled him with all his talk.

Monday he set out again and he had extra good luck that week. The load was heavy, and it was late in the evening before he came back to the blockhouse on Friday. There was no light in the house. Gustav should have been there, since he had started out a day before Olav.

But something was wrong. Olav could hear the dogs inside the blockhouse howling and barking as he came closer. His own dogs began barking too, but there was still no light inside the house. It was very strange, and Olav felt scared. He took his time with the dogs to give Gustav time to wake up and come outside to meet him. But then he noticed that there was no smoke coming up the chimney and quite a lot of snow had settled in front of the door.

At last he went in. It was pretty dark and he got out his matches. It was just as cold in the house as outside. The dogs jumped on him, howling. Olav took off his heavy clothes and lit a candle. Gustav was in bed with his back to Olav.

"Gustav!" he called. No movement. It didn't take him long to understand that Gustav was dead.

At first he would not let it be true. He made a fire in the stove and cut some ice for the pot. The whole water barrel outside was a solid block of ice, and it had always been the duty of the first man home to thaw some ice. Olav even began scolding Gustav for neglecting his duties.

He didn't want to look at Gustav. As long as he didn't, he could pretend that the man was asleep, that he would soon wake up. He fed the hungry dogs, told them that Gustav was drunk, that that was the reason why they never got their food. He knew it was a lie, but he felt he had to say something.

He kept up the pretense that Gustav was asleep. He knew how miserable he would be once he admitted that his partner was dead. Suddenly he felt utterly exhausted, tumbled into his own bed, and fell asleep.

I remember Olav made a pause in his story at that point, staring at us with those faraway eyes without recognizing us, turning at last to the sheriff again with pleading in his voice as he went on: "You don't know such loneliness, Sheriff. You don't know that darkness. You don't understand how a man can make himself believe something he knows is not true, something which is obviously a lie." With a deep sigh, Olav went on with his story.

When he got up the following morning, Olav made hot cereal for both of them.

"Do you want some?" he called out to Gustav. There was

no answer, since the other man was dead, but Olav didn't want
to let Gustav see that he knew it.

That was Saturday morning, and Olav decided to keep Gustav in the house until Sunday night. He wanted some company
over the weekend at least, then he could bury him Monday
morning and set out on his usual round, so he wouldn't have to
sit alone at home feeling miserable. He decided to check Gustav's
traps, too. There must be plenty of foxes in them, and he would
bring them back to Gustav.

Nonsense! he told himself. Gustav was dead, what would
he do with the foxes?

Suddenly he decided to have a look at the dead man. Gustav
was lying hunched up in bed with his legs pulled up. He looked
just as if he were sitting in a chair. He was frozen stiff, of course,
but the face looked as if Gustav were laughing. Olav lifted him
up and put him down on a chair by the table, then he sat down
to his lonely breakfast.

Olav talked to the dead man as he ate his food. He felt that
he had to give Gustav the answer to all the things they had been
talking about the weekend before, about the soul, about religion
and immortality. Gustav had said he did not believe he would
go to heaven, he didn't know where it was or what it looked
like. It was hard to answer a man like that, but Olav went on
talking.

Gustav just sat there laughing. That was the way he looked
anyway. And Olav talked to him, otherwise it would have been
too lonely. He supplied the answers himself, told himself all the
things he thought Gustav would have answered. That way he
could talk back again and forget that his friend was dead. It was
hard to keep up, of course. There wasn't really much to talk
about, and Olav didn't feel like saying the same things over and
over again.

In the evening he took Gustav outside. He put him on a
sleigh and pulled him over to a small cliff behind the house.
First he put the body down in the snow and then covered it with
stones, lots of stones piled neatly on top of the body. He didn't
want wolves and bears to eat his friend Gustav.

It was a strange week. Olav looked after his own traps first, then Gustav's. And he took all four dogs along. He didn't want any of them to stay at home and howl as soon as he approached the house again, coming back for a lonely weekend.

When he got back the following Sunday, Olav was very tired and decided to stay in the house for a whole week. He had to soften up all the skins and put them up for drying. There was a lot to do, and he was alone with the job.

As he sat by himself in the blockhouse, Olav began thinking that it had been better, after all, when he had Gustav at the table with him, even though he was dead. Now Gustav was outside, freezing in the terrible cold, poor man. That was all nonsense, of course, he thought. But still, he was so utterly alone and -- well, Gustav wasn't really buried, after all, just covered with stones. And Olav had to sit there and eat all alone. He had to go out by himself, look after the traps by himself, he had to feed the dogs by himself, and now one of them was having puppies on top of it all. Gustav had been looking forward to that.

It was nobody's business, Olav thought. Since he was all alone, it didn't really concern anybody, and it was his intention all the time to put Gustav out again, to bury him decently. But just while it was so terribly dark, for a little while only.

In short, he took Gustav in again. He regretted it once he had him inside, but then it was done and he had to stick to it. When he had him sitting there on the other side of the table, things seemed a little brighter. Olav talked to him and went on answering for him. He knew Gustav pretty well, by then, so it was just like playing with dolls. And he was sure Gustav would never have objected to it.

They had quite a good time together, he felt. Olav prepared food for both of them and set a place for Gustav. He even served him, and he got angry when Gustav didn't eat and he had to give the food to the puppies. He pretended to be angry because Gustav was so finicky about his food -- that was part of the game.

When he went to bed that night, he left Gustav sitting by the table. That was a great mistake, because he woke up in the middle of the night and Gustav was moving! He could have sworn to it that the body was moving. He was wide awake in a second -- and here is the strange part: he really wanted to be afraid that Gustav was moving. He knew all the time that the body was only thawing, but he did not want to admit it. If he did, he would have to give up the game of make-believe, of pretending that Gustav was still alive.

When Gustav died, he had been all hunched up with one arm bent forward a little so Olav could put it on the table edge for support. Gustav had looked quite natural that way. It was this arm which began thawing, that was the whole explanation. Olav had to have some heat in the house to thaw the stiffly frozen foxes, but he should not have let Gustav thaw with them. That night he was so scared he could hardly move. He even said the Lord's Prayer, although he really knew all the time that the thing was quite natural, that the body was only softening. And toward morning he calmed down again.

"Come along, my fine friend," he said to Gustav as he got up. "You are going out in the snow again. You are all through scaring decent people."

And once more he covered Gustav with stones before he set out on his round. He worked out a new system with the rounds. First he looked after half of his own traps to the south and half of Gustav's to the north. That way he came back to the blockhouse twice a week. And not for a second did he dream of doing Gustav out of his share of the catch.

Every time he got back to the lonely house, he felt drawn to that stone grave again. The urge got too strong and after a couple of weeks he gave in again. He brought Gustav into the house and put him down at the table once more. He served him his food as before, and the puppies got what was left on the plate. If anybody sees me, they'll think I'm crazy, Olav thought. But he didn't care. He just kept talking all the time, for Gustav and himself. If he stopped for a moment, the cold silence would come between them again and he would have to admit that his friend was dead, and he didn't want to do that.

When the light began coming back to Greenland, a little more of it every day, Olav thought he would get over it. Once he could really get a good look at Gustav, it would be too crazy to carry a dead man back and forth. He had seen too many friends and fellow trappers die to be impressed by death, but everything was different with Gustav. Every time he returned to the house, he was determined not to take him back again, but he always found some excuse. Actually, even in death, Gustav had such an influence on Olav in life that Olav couldn't ignore him. It began to irritate him a little.

There was hardly a weekend when he did not have Gustav in the house with him. The body got a little worn from all the handling, of course. The sun was getting warmer every day and sometimes it would shine right in his face. He noticed for the first time that Gustav's skin was a dark yellow. He was furious with him, telling him that he was dead and should stay dead. He didn't want to see him again, he shouted to the body. This is the last time you'll be in a room with me, he yelled at Gustav.

Gustav just sat there grinning at him. He had been a little too close to the fire and his mouth had sunk a little, making his grin even more gruesome. Olav knew that he was sure to go out of his head altogether if he kept this routine until the warmer weather set in. Gustav would thaw completely and his body would have an unbearable stench. But how could he stop it?

One day he noticed a snow sparrow outside and he knew he had to do something. The bird was a sure sign of spring, the fox trapping was over for the winter, the ice would soon break up, and the Blue Whale would return to take them back to Denmark.

He was afraid, he was really scared when he returned to the house with the last traps. Scared of Gustav, scared of his ghost -- for he was really a ghost, the only difference being that Gustav didn't walk around by himself, because Olav carried him. It was just like when he was alive, he could make Olav do things he would never have done voluntarily by himself.

The idea came to him all of a sudden. He knew what he had to do -- and he knew that it was the only right thing to do. He took Gustav in and went on talking to him as if he had nothing up his sleeve. He smiled to himself when he told Gustav about all the things they would do the next day, just to reassure his friend. After a while, he told Gustav that he had to go outside for some more coal for the fire. He had his gun outside, of course. He didn't close the door all the way, left it open just a little crack. Gustav couldn't call out and complain of the cold, poor man. But Olav knew he was going to fool him this time.

He sneaked back to the house with the gun in his hand, ready loaded. It took him at least an hour to get the barrel of the gun through the crack and get it in the right position. Gustav sat there just where Olav had put him. He had his back to Olav, but he was turned a little sideways, just enough to let Olav see his smile -- a disgusting grin which wasn't really like him at all.

This time he was alive, Olav felt, but he had had enough of him now. And he cocked the gun. Taking good aim was a slow business. Even if he was a dead man, it was, after all, a friend that Olav was going to shoot. Just as he was going to pull the trigger, Gustav moved. The arm was getting soft again. It was hard to shoot him while he was still moving.

But Olav had to rid himself of Gustav. Suddenly he got furious with Gustav for trying to scare him even at the very last moment. And then he shot.

A deafening roar shook the small blockhouse. The whole back of the head was blown to pieces. At last he was really dead and would never again visit Olav. After all, Olav would never carry a man with half a head into the house.

He buried his friend the real way this time and made a wooden cross for the grave. It felt good to be alone. Nobody to pay any attention to. He didn't miss Gustav. His friend was dead now, true enough, and it was a great pity, but there was nothing he could do about it. Quietly and peacefully, Olav prepared for the trip home. The Blue Whale would come any day now, he knew.

During the voyage home, Olav wanted to throw himself overboard, he said. The only thing which kept him from it was the thought that people would only think the worse of him. Nobody spoke to him on that trip back home. He had a cabin alone by himself, nobody would eat with him or have anything to do with him.

"I knew what they thought of me and I knew what would happen," Olav finished. "And I was right. This morning the whole police force came to get me. We only came home yesterday and I walked alone to my house then, but today you needed four policemen to bring me down here.

"I am no murderer, Sheriff! I only used my gun to make Gustav leave me in peace once he was dead. I only killed a dead man. There is no law against that! Or is there? You tell me."

Olav was taken back to his cell that night and in prison they must have called him a murderer, told him that he had killed his best friend. That proved too much for him. Olav had always been a strong man, a good and honest once, but this was more than he could take. All that winter he must have been on the borderline, and that night he finally lost his mind.

An autopsy quickly confirmed his story. The medical examination showed that the body had been dead for some time and frozen stiff when it was shot in the head. Olav's name was cleared, there could be no question of murder, and the sheriff announced that no charge would be raised.

But it was much too late. Olav was incurably insane by then. He didn't understand what the sheriff told him and kept up a constant, incoherent muttering to himself. He was brought to an asylum and he is still there.

He was one of the strong and good men in the Artic who couldn't take the unusual, the event outside his routine. He didn't have much to fall back on, he didn't read much, perhaps he didn't think much, and he couldn't stand being alone.

But who knows, maybe the same thing would have happened to him if he had lived down here in more civilized regions.

STORY OUTLINE

I. Olav and his partner, Thomas Vold, break up after many years of trapping together.

II. Olav finds a new partner, Gustav Krakau, who is enthusiastic, and who brings books and other items trappers normally do not have.

III. Gustav learns quickly and Olav sees new wonders through his eyes. They trap separately north and south from their cabin. Olav looks forward to talking and listening to Gustav on weekends.

IV. Gustav becomes ill, and when Olav returns from a trip he finds him dead in bed.

V. Olav fixes supper, pretending for a few minutes more that his friend is alive. He tells the dogs his partner is drunk. He also fixes breakfast the next morning and again asks him if he wishes to eat.

VI. Olav notes that Gustav is frozen in a sitting position with a grin on his face; he sits him in a chair propped on his arm, and continues pretending that he is alive, having breakfast with him.

VII. He almost forgets that his friend is really dead during the day, but that night he wraps him in a tarp and lays stones and ice over him.

VIII. After a week running both trap lines, Olav decides to spend a week in the cabin working on the fur. He misses Gustav and decides to bring him back to the cabin and prop him up at the table again.

IX. Gustav starts to thaw that night, moving, and

scaring Olav. He is returned to the snow bank the next day.

X. Many weekends Olav brings Gustav back inside again. He can not help himself, he is so lonely. But he is also mad at himself for having to do it.

XI. He has pretended that his friend is alive so long, that even with the body beginning to sag in the heat and to discolor, he cannot consider him dead to bury him.

XII. Olav decides to leave a rifle outside and shoot Gustav in the head, thus officially making him dead -- which he does.

XIII. When the boat comes to pick them up, the Captain orders the grave opened and the body exhumed. They find he has been shot.

XIV. When they get back Olav is arrested. The coroner notes that Gustav was dead when shot. Olav is exonerated, but he goes insane and is locked up the rest of his life.

THE MACKENZIE RIVER GHOST

as told by Ernest Thompson Seton[1]

Introduction

In the late 1800's, some eminent scientists headed by Sir Oliver Lodge founded a Society of Psychical Research to ascertain if there was such a thing as a ghost in the ordinary sense of the word. They offered to investigate every supposed ghost and to do it in the calm cold way of exact science.

Hundreds of instances were sent them; and at least 99 percent of the ghosts were totally dissipated under the disintegrating white light of the scientific approach. But a few there were that would not dissipate, that defied all attempts to explain them away. Among them was the ghost of the Mackenzie River.

In his early days -- that is in the 1880's -- Seton lived in the Northwest and knew many employees of the Hudson Bay Company. Among them was one bluff old Scotchman, Roderick MacFarlane. After many years, MacFarlane was retired and lived in Winnipeg on a small pension. Each time Seton was in that city -- about once a year -- Mac and he would have a pleasant reunion over a good dinner.

---

[1] Reprinted by permission from *Trail and Campfire Stories* by Julia M. Seton, Copyright 1940, 1944, 1947, 1950, 1965.

"Mac," Seton asked, "did you ever hear anything about the Mackenzie River ghost?"

"What ghost?" said he.

"A ghost that came in broad daylight to some men on the ice of the Mackenzie River. The story was told by a Hudson Bay Company Factor." [2]

"Humph," said Mac, "that factor was me. But Lodge and his group didn't tell it right, nor at full length. I'll give you the facts right now if you like. You can do as you please with it after I'm gone. Do you want to hear it?"

"I sure do," said Seton. "Go on. Tell it as long as you please."

And this is the tale as MacFarlane told it that night:

* * * * *

Away back in the 1860's, the Company thought that there was a good chance of a successful trading post at the mouth of the Mackenzie, since this was Eskimo as well as Indian country and there was no post with 400 miles in any direction. So, with Sandy MacDonald for a helper, I was outfitted for the job. When summer came, we went to the Mackenzie Delta; and then, turning west, we selected the mouth of Peel River, where we built a couple of log houses, gathered a great pile of driftwood, and were ready for any fur trade that came along.

Next spring, when the river opened, we had a visitor by canoe -- a young fellow named Middleton, about twenty-two years of age, a graduate of Oxford. He came equipped with letters from the High Council of our Company. He was filled with missionary zeal, his one hope and dream being to preach the Gospel to the Eskimos. He had no knowledge of the Eskimos or of their language; but he was undaunted by these difficulties, for he felt he was the chosen vessel to bring back the tidings of

---

[2] A factor was a highly placed and very responsible manager of the great fur trading company which literally ruled the back country of Canada from the 1670's to the 1870's. As such, a factor was highly respected for his integrity.

salvation.

He was the most impractical, helpless creature I ever saw in the wilds. He knew nothing but his Oxford and his Bible. He seemed to us sometimes like a madman. But he came with letters from the boss, so we had to take him into our family.

Yes, we received him first only on the strength of the letters; but after a month or two, we were ready to accept him on account of his personal worth and charm. Far from strong, and troubled with a hacking cough, he was nevertheless always ready to do his share, and more than his share, of the work. He was the one who got up first in the morning to light the fire and start the breakfast. He was the one to wash the dishes or scrub the dirty floor. It might be a zero blizzard outdoors, but he was the one who volunteered first to go out after more firewood.

He had brought a fiddle with him. He played well and had a string of good songs, and many a long, dreary winter night he whiled away for us, with his music and fun. I tell you we learned to love that poor fellow like a little brother.

But there was something sad in it all -- that cough. It grew worse, and in spite of his bright spirits and cheerful soul, he was plainly fading away. Toward the end of the winter, he was so thin and weak that he couldn't go out of the door without getting frostbite. His cough was terrible and he was spitting blood. Still he was bright, cheerful, and hopeful, and worked steadily at his Eskimo Grammar.

Then came days when he couldn't leave his bunk. One night he called us to him and said to me: "Mac, you know I'm not long for this world; I felt my Saviour calling me home. You fellows have been so good to me I want to ask one last favor."

"There isn't anything in our power you can't ask," I said for both.

"When my soul goes on," he says, "I don't want my poor body to be thrust into a hole in the ground like some animal. Won't you please bury me in consecrated ground?" [3]

---

[3] Consecrated ground would be the sanctified cemetery plot next to a church.

"If it costs my last dollar and my life, I give you my word as a man that I will carry out your wishes," was my answer, and Sandy and I took his poor thin hands in ours, and we gave our solemn promise.

I tell you we were blubbering like two babies. But he wasn't; he was bright and happy.

A month later, the end came. He passed away, happy and peaceful.

The nearest consecrated burying ground was at Fort Resolution, 400 miles up the Mackenzie River and fully 500 from our post. We had no right to leave our post now, so we wrapped the corpse in caribou hides. Then with our axes we chopped a grave three feet deep in the ice that never melts on the Mackenzie Mouth.

When he was laid in it, we filled it level with water; and within a few hours, it was one solid mass of ice, level with the rest.

We put a little marker at each end of the place, which was all we could do at that time. I tell you living with that kind brave soul had done more for me than any book or sermon ever did. And Sandy and I just prayed for a way to carry out our promise.

Well, sir, it was full two years we had to wait, and we surely felt bad about it. But the chance came. The High Council of our Company sent orders to close up the post and travel at once with all books and records to Fort Resolution, where we were to report to the Superintendent of the District.

This gave us the chance we had looked for. We had two sleds, each with a team of fine big Husky dogs. On one sled we loaded the books and records of the post, our camping outfit, and grub for ourselves and dogs. On the other, we loaded the corpse which we were able to dig out after a couple of hours chopping. Sandy drove one team; an Indian who had been working for us drove the other. I, the boss, trotted ahead to break the trail.

I tell you it was a funeral like nothing else before -- a double funeral. First, it was the end of Peel Post. You see, we knew there was no chance of rival traders by land; but we hadn't reckoned on the whalers, who came by sea and wintered not far

away. They did some whaling, but their best trade was in fur
with the Eskimos.

So we left a lot of valuable stuff in the cabins and nailed
them up to keep off the bears. We knew no Eskimo or Indian
would steal anything -- they never do -- and when the summer
came, the boat brigade would salvage all.

But our big thought was the other sled. We must keep faith
with the dead man. And away we went in easy stages to cover
five hundred miles of ice and snow.

The Mackenzie River is two miles wide at the mouth. It
has gravel banks and runs through a wide plain with only level
snow till the black line of the forest begins, three to ten miles
away on each side.

The best traveling for the sleds is up the middle of the ice,
for there the wind has blown the snow away, and the ice is clear
and firm for the runners.

So each morning we set out up the middle of the river ice,
trotting along for maybe twenty miles. Then we made our noon
halt. Driving to the nearest gravel bank, we hauled up onto the
level plain. But there is no wood short of the pine forest miles
away across the deep soft snow; so, in order to avoid this hard
trip, we always carried on the front of one sled enough firewood
to melt snow and boil it for our tea, and then a little more to
cook our bacon.

After an hour's rest, we set out again for twenty miles more.

Then at night, we would leave the river, and break our way
to the forest, where we made a comfortable camp with plenty of
wood. And I tell you, I always kept the funeral sled by my bed,
for I felt under a solemn vow to protect that. In the morning we
gathered a new bundle of wood for the noon and set out again
on the ice.

This was our daily routine for about a week. Then one day
at noon, after we had driven up on the gravel bank ten feet above
the river, I found we had lost some of our firewood. There wasn't
enough to melt a kettle of snow and then cook our meal. So I
said to the Indian: "Take the ax and chop through the river ice.
If we can get to the water, that will save half the wood we need."

The Indian chopped and chopped till he was down the length of the ax handle. But still he was not through the ice. He called, and Sandy went down to see if there was any show of the water.

Soon he shouted back; "No good." I said: "Then look for an air-hole," and went down to help the search.

All of a sudden, we heard loud cries from a human voice on the river bank ten feet above us.

" *Allez! Allez! Allez!*" it shouted. Then "*Marchez! Marchez!*"

We did not suppose there was a human being within hundreds of miles of us. But again came the ringing "*Allez! Allez! Allez!*" -- the French that one always uses in ordering and driving the dogs harnessed before the sled.

In haste and amazement, we rushed up the bank and into view of our outfit. Here was the wide level expanse of snow bright in the winter sun, and *not a sign of a human being in sight except ourselves.* But there, laying a groveling heap, were the ten big fierce Husky dogs, growling and rumbling, their eyes glowing, their hair bristling. The tracks showed plainly that taking advantage of our absence, the very first time they were left alone with the corpse, these hungry, half-tame wolves decided to attack and devour the body. But the moment they touched it, that ringing voice of command was heard driving them back in terror.

"Who spoke?" I asked almost in a whisper.

Sandy replied, also in a whisper: "Well, it was a white man's voice, for an Indian can't say '*Marche*'; he says '*Mush*.' "

"Who spoke?" I said to the Indian. He pointed with emphasis to the corpse and added in a low tone: "His voice."

I tell you we never took any chances after that -- night and day some one of us always was next to the body. We felt under a vow to keep it safe and carry out our promise.

Day after day and night after night we went on with the same routine, some days making forty miles, but on many days of blizzard storm making little or nothing.

Finally we arrived at the upper reaches of the Mackenzie, where timber was plentiful, and where islands with trees were right in the river; so we had no trouble finding good campsites.

One evening we came on an island covered with timber, right handy, and decided to camp there. Its shores were clay cut-banks about ten feet high. We left our two sleds on the ice, but Sandy and I climbed up. The Indian caught the dogs one by one, and we hauled them up onto the level top. Here we turned them loose, for I knew they would not leave the fire, and that ten foot drop was as good as a fence all around.

About nine o'clock, I was smoking my pipe before turning in, when I heard a strange far-away call on the wooded shore.

"*Ye-hoo-ooo-ooo!*"

I started up, for it was repeated.

"*Ye-hoo-ooo-ooo!*"

At first I thought it was a horned owl, or maybe a wolf call. But again it came with human intonation.

"*Ye-hoo-ooo-ooo!*"

"Say, Sandy, there's some one out there, a lost traveler." So I went to the edge of the island, and shouted back.

"Hallo! Hallo, there! Who are you?" There was no answer, even to a second call, so I came back to the fire. Very soon again there came:

"*Ye-hoo-ooo!*"

I went to the edge of the timber, and shouted: "Who are you? Why don't you come on? Can't you see the fire?"

There was no answer to this, and I said to my pal:

"Say, Sandy, I don't feel comfortable about leaving our charge on the ice. The dogs can't get near it; but anyway, let's put it up a tree."

So we three went down in the darkness; and after much trouble, got our burden safe up a thick bushy tree. We heard no more calls in the night.

Next morning, as my helper was packing and making ready for a start, I prowled around in the snow and on the ice. There I learned from the tracks that all the previous evening, and maybe for a couple of days before, we had been followed by a wolverine. Our charge would have been unprotected by the dogs and exposed to the wolverine, which certainly would have found and disfigured it, had we not acted on the weird warning that came in time.

After that, our journey continued with little incident till near Christmas, when we reached Fort Resolution.

There I turned over my charge to the Archbishop, who laid it by the altar in the church, promising to attend to all proper ceremonies as soon as feasible -- which meant as soon as the springtime made it possible to dig a grave.

That night we three travelers slept in the rampasture, which is the name of the bunkhouse in a Hudson Bay Fort.

The moon was full, shining on the snow, and, through the window, lighted up the place well. About ten o'clock I was awakened with a sudden feeling of alertness. I sat up as unsleepy as could be, and there right opposite to me were Sandy and the Indian both sitting up.

Then there came on me an overwhelming feeling of bliss, of happiness complete; and in the gloom, I thought I saw on Sandy's face the same expression of rapture. I do not know any word to describe the sensation but "ecstasy." It gradually faded away. We gazed at each other and at the door and at nowhere.

I said: "Sandy, did you see anything?"

"No," he whispered.

"Did you feel anything, Sandy?"

"I did," he said. "I was filled with joy."

"What was it?" I asked.

In a low but certain voice, he said: "He came in gratitude to us for carrying out our promise. Thank God we didn't fail him! We have surely had our reward."

STORY OUTLINE

I. Seton's visit with Roderick MacFarlane sets the stage for the telling of a true ghost story.

II. Roderick MacFarlane and Sandy Macdonald

are sent from Ft. Resolution 400 miles down the Mackenzie River to the Arctic Ocean and then 100 miles along the coast to the Peel River, there to build a post to trade for fur with the Eskimos.

III. The next spring they are unhappy to receive a young fellow named Middleton with commands from Hudson Bay Company officials that they take care of this person while he works on translating the Bible into Eskimo.

IV. He turns out to be very helpful and a good friend. But he becomes very ill. They promise to grant his last request before he dies -- it is to be buried in sanctified ground.

V. To complete their promise they will have to transport the body 500 miles back to Ft. Resolution. Two years later they are ordered to close the post. That winter they exhume the body and start the dog sled journey with an Indian helper.

VI. The Mackenzie River is two miles wide, with the tree line 3 to 5 miles from the river. Each night they must make the trip to the trees to have firewood. They bring enough wood on the sleds for their noon meal.

VII. After the first week they come to a gravel bank at about noon. The dogs and sleds are driven up on the bank and the men leave them there, returning to the river ice to cut a hole for water.

VIII. While on the river they hear a human voice shout ALLEZ! ALLEZ! ALLEZ! then MARCHEZ!, the white man's command to a dog team. When they rush back to the sleds they find that the wild husky dogs are cowering in fear, but the tracks show that they have come up to the body to eat it. There is no one around; the Indian thinks it was the dead man's voice that protected the body.

IX. One evening they come to an island, ideal for camping. They bring the dogs up the steep bank to keep them away from the body, which they leave below.

X. That night they hear someone shout "Ye-hoo-ooo-oooo!" several times. Rushing down to the river with burning torches, they bring the body up the bank, putting it in a tree. The next day they see that a wolverine almost got the body, but was suddenly scared off!

XI. They finally make it to Ft. Resolution safely and turn the body over to the priest. That night when asleep in the rampasture (the bunkhouse), MacFarlane suddenly wakes up with a very pleasant feeling surrounding him. He notices the other two are awake also. The feeling fades, and Sandy states what they instinctively know, that it was surely their friend who had returned to thank them.

THE DEATH OF THE OLD LION

as told by Ernest Thompson Seton[1]

Introduction

Ernest Thompson Seton is remembered for his many contributions as a founder of the Boy Scout movement in the United States, as a great naturalist, as a writer and a master story teller. A true story which he related is a remarkable tale from Africa that took place in the late 1800's -- the story of a proud lion and the fate which he chose for himself!

* * * * *

It was a big burly negro, a Zulu named Em-Vubu from South Africa, who told us this tale. He had come to New York as a stoker on a tramp steamer. He spoke English fairly well and was gifted with that peculiar insight into the minds of animals that is often found in primitives and especially the black-skinned race of the Voodoo cult in Africa.

Originally he had been a farmhand on the ranch of a Boer in the open country beyond Orange River. His job each morning

[1] Reprinted by permission from *Trail and Campfire Stories* by Julia M. Seton, Copyright 1940, 1944, 1947, 1950, 1965.

had been to round up the horses into the kraal.

Through a number of accidental circumstances, he had learned something about his master's activities that would certainly have put the man in wrong with the British authorities and probably landed him in jail. So the Boer made up his mind to get rid of the Zulu.

Em-vubu brought in the horse herd as usual one morning and announced to the Dutchman: "Horses is in kraal."

The Boer went to the kraal, looked the herd over, and said with severity: "Where is my little bay mare?"

"Dere ain't no more horses," replied the Zulu. "All is in de kraal."

"Don't you tell me that!" shouted the farmer. "I want that little bay mare I bought the other day."

"I don't know nothin' 'bout no bay mare," said the Zulu.

"You better learn something quick!" replied the Boer. And, taking down a big jambok whip, the Boer cracked it fiercely and shouted: "Looka, here, you black brute; get out and find that mare. If you come back without her, I'll cut you to pieces at the whipping post!" And he cracked the whip like pistol shots.

Now, Em-vubu knew that there was trouble ahead unless he could find a stray horse, so he prepared for a long journey. He put a lump of dry meat in his rucksack, hung a bottle of water at his side, sought out a good kaross or sleeping blanket, then, armed only with a knob-kerry or club, set out for his trek.

He did not believe in the story of the bay mare, but he tramped out far from the settlement into the wild karoo, looking for a horse or a track of a horse. But nothing was to be seen.

At night, he was many miles away and sought out a sheltering bank in a coulee and there he made a fire and slept.

Next morning, he went on; and still farther on the third day. He was now on the far karoo, and ahead he discerned one of those African hills called a kopje. He made for this, sure that it would give him a good look-out, a survey of the desert around.

One side was a long slope, the other a perpendicular drop of 300 or 400 feet. Up the ascending side he tramped and easily reached the top. Here he had a wonderful view of the whole country.

He scanned it near and far, wondering if it was possibly true that the boss had a horse out here.

He saw no sign of a living thing until he looked backward over his own trail a mile or more. There he saw some dark object that seemed to move slowly, some wild animal, or maybe a horse.

He watched it intently. It came very slowly but at last was near enough to be distinguished. Without doubt, it was a huge lion. It was coming in his direction.

Now he watched with double interest and at length realized that the lion was *following his trail*. His concern now was at boiling point. He looked for some way of refuge or escape.

On the top of the hill were three ragged thorn bushes, not very high, but rough and strong. He selected the biggest of these and climbed up, hoping to be beyond reach if not wholly hidden.

The lion approached very slowly, and the Negro saw now that it was not on his trail, but merely following the same general line of travel.

As the lion reached the slope of the kopje, it went even more slowly, and now the Negro could see that it was a very old and sick lion, so old and sick that it could barely climb the hill. His tail was dragging on the ground, his ribs and backbone were sticking out, his head seemed too heavy for him to lift. He had to lie down and rest three or four times in the ascent. He trembled as he came.

He passed under the Negro without pausing or looking up, dragging his feeble frame a few inches at as time. He reached the edge of the cliff, and here he lay down for a long time.

Then, at length, he rose on his braced and tottering limbs, swung his great shaggy head this way and that, as he seemed to scan the plain, took a deep breath, and let out a long lion-moan --- "*mmmmm.*"

The effort exhausted him, and he flopped down on his breast. But the end of his tail wagged a little, showing that he was pleased.

A rest of half an hour revived him. Once more he stood on his shaky legs, gazed to the right and left, and managed to utter a louder, stronger moan --- "*MMMMMMMMMMMM.*"

Again it was too much for his strength, and he lay on his belly for another long rest. But his tail vibrated more than before; he was feeling happier.

Another long wait, and the old warrior rose to his feet again. He looked over the world below him, took three or four deep hard breaths, "Hah hah hah hah," then put all his remaining force into a last attempt, and got out a vibrant "*R-O-A-R-R-R-R*," a faint reminder of a lion's hunting roar.

When he found that he had done this, had at last voiced a real roar something like those he used to do, he leaped from that high precipice and was dashed to death and destruction, down, down, 400 feet below.

He knew that his days were over, his hunting ended, his strength gone. He could no loger live the life of a lion. If he kept on, he must live the life of a jackal, on carrion, offal, dung, insects, filth. On the other hand, he could come to this hill that he had known in the days of his strength, here view the great kingdom that once had been his, and in sight of it all, he could *die like a lion*.

That was what he had elected to do.

EPILOGUE

The Animal Kingdom is full of stories of animals who have given their lives that their off-spring might survive, or in sacrifice for a human master. This is the only story that I know of in which an animal commits suicide rather than face a miserable, slow, and humiliating death. For other unusual animal stories the reader is referred to Seton's great book, *Great Historic Animals*, with stories of 19 animals that lived in history.

STORY OUTLINE

I. In this story Seton relates the true adventure which was told him by a South African native, a Zulu named Em-vubu.

II. Working as a farm hand, he was being mistreated by the mean owner. In fact he was accused of losing a mare, which the native knew was not lost. He was told to go into the bush until he found it.

III. The native packed all that he could, hoping that he might find a stray horse to bring back and appease the farm owner.

IV. He traveled far out into the brush. Several days later he came to the edge of a large cliff, the edge of a geological fault, which consisted of a slope on one side, but a large vertical drop on the other.

V. He hoped to be able to look out from this cliff and find a horse. But when he looked back he could see that a lion was following him!

VI. He had no way to defend himself against a lion. The best he could do was to hide in a large thorn bush.

VII. When the lion came close, he saw that it was an old lion which was barely able to walk.

VIII. The old lion passed by him and went to the cliff edge, looking out over the domain he once ruled.

IX. The climb up the gentle slope exhausted the lion. After resting he made several attempts to roar. He had to rest after each try.

X. Finally he let out a loud R-O-A-R-R-R, a

reminder of the hunting roars which he used to call out with. Having accomplished this, the lion leaped to his death off the cliff.

XI. The lion wanted to die, remembering the old glorious days, rather than having to live off of scraps and rotten meat left over by others, now that he was old and feeble.

THE ICE WALKER

as told by Grey Owl [1]

Introduction

Grey Owl was one of the unusual breed of Englishmen who became so infatuated with the natural life in the wilds of Canada that they immigrated and became woodsmen. Grey Owl went so far as to assume the identity of an Indian. He was adopted into an Indian tribe and given the name *Wa-sha-quon-asin*. He had the talent of writing about his many experiences and his epic stories of the vast North Land, of the men -- both Indians and white -- of the animals that live there, and of the trees and rivers which are its sentinels and highways, make the Canadian wilderness come alive for us. Living in a primitive and isolated area, Grey Owl once encountered this story of adventure in the Northland.

* * * * *

For some time past I had heard the man coming. The tock, tock of his pole as he tapped the ice had been audible from a

[1] Reprinted by permission of Macmillan of Canada, A Division of Gage Publishing Limited, from *Tales of an Empty Cabin*, copyright 1936 by Grey Owl, as a story originally titled "Nemesis."

distance of perhaps a mile, the sound magnified and carried far and wide, as is the way with a blow struck on glare ice.

This testing ice by sound is often necessary during the early part of Winter, the pole being swung naturally and easily in the stride, the end being allowed to drop with its full weight at every fourth step, much as a drum major wields his staff.

The timing of the strokes in this case was such that the traveler seemed to strike the ice at every other step; the steps of one who is unhurried, walking slowly, but steadily. And as he walked came the tap tap, of the pole, regular as the "tuck" of the drum of marching infantry. It was late Fall, and I knew the ice to be bad, especially at this place, a large shallow lake bottomed with a treacherous, gaseous slime, which spelt death for him who should break through and be sucked into the hungry maw of the shifting ooze. The lake itself was walled in by the towering black palisades of a gloomy spruce forest, into which no ray of sunlight ever penetrated, and was backed by miles of almost impassable swamps.

A desolate region, and one that I avoided as much as possible in my goings and comings on the trap lines.

Suddenly remembering my duties as probable host to a tired man, I stirred up the smouldering fire, put the cold tea on afresh and endeavored to make some semblance of a meal out of the remains of the lunch I had just eaten. As I so busied myself, I wondered a little what event could bring a stranger into my hunting ground, at a time when the Fall hunt was in full swing.

My temporary camping place was not visible from the lake but the smoke was plain to be seen, and I knew that the voyageur would not fail to turn in and stop awhile, as is the custom with those who travel in the Wilderness. So I sat by my fire and smoked, and anxiously awaited the newcomer's arrival, for something in the manner of his coming indicated (for a lifetime on the trail trains the faculties to a degree of perception in such matter), that he who had penetrated so far within my boundaries was no ordinary trapper. There seemed, for one thing, to be some peculiar quality in this man's method of feeling out the ice; in the first place there was his unusual action of striking at every third step as though marking time on a line of march, and then the additional resonance he produced by the unusually heavy blows he struck, as though he carried a weightier staff than was commonly used. And over and above that was the changeless, unbroken rhythm of the strokes, which were as measured and uniform as the ticking of some gigantic clock.

And his slow, unfaltering strides seemed to suggest a dogged persistence, as of a man with a mission to fulfill, and a man, moreover, not easily swerved from his purpose. Onward he marched, his every step timed by the steady, persistent tap of the pole, tock, tock, tock, until the regularity and monotony of the sounds exercised an almost hypnotic influence on my mind as I sat and waited. He seemed long in coming, walking slowly as he did, yet so persistently that he should have long ago arrived. And then quite suddenly I realized that the sound was now beyond the stopping place and that the wayfarer, whoever he might be, had ignored the presence of my camp, in spite of the smoke and the light sleigh in full view on the shore, and had passed on. An unusual, nay, an unheard of proceeding amongst bushmen, and unaccountable unless the man be blind, or an enemy.

There does not live the man of any character who has not made at least one enemy in his lifetime, and this last thought stuck in my mind.

I went out onto the ice, but the passerby was already out of sight beyond a point, for the lake was one of irregular shores and many deep bays and inlets, in which concealment for purposes of ambush would have been an easy matter. And I could still hear plainly the measured stroke of the pole, a sound which, from being merely eerie, had now become ominous, seeming to tap forth a challenge, or a threat.

I hastened out to the center of the lake for a fuller view, and still saw no one, so I returned to my camp, extinguished my fire, and quickly arming myself, started in pursuit. I traveled at a dog-trot the usual gait on glare ice, taking, as I did so, full advantage of the excellent cover that the broken character of the shore line afforded, having as a guide to the line of march of my quarry, the steady, never ceasing rapping on the ice.

For an hour or more I followed the intruder. There being now no necessity for testing the ice where one had passed ahead of me, I lost no time, yet great as was my speed, and slow as his appeared to be, found that I could in no wise catch up to him.

In spite of his apparently leisurely progress he seemed to be able to keep his distance. The sound swung off to my right, and following it, I saw that the chase had taken me into a deep and apparently endless bay, of which, up to that time, I had had no knowledge. Down this I pursued the elusive, baffling tattoo for miles, always trotting, and the invisible stranger always walking with his measured steps.

Almost it was as though the man carried a huge metronome, or that the creature itself were not a human being but a robot. Grimly determined to get to the bottom of this mystery, I followed mile after mile, regardless of where this will-o'-the-wisp of sound was leading me; over wide expanses of lake, through narrow gorges, along winding forest-bordered streams, but always on ice, and ever to the accompaniment of that unvarying and monotonous rapping.

Eventually I found myself in a part of my hunting ground that I had never before set eyes on, a barren desolation of blow-down, burnt lands, and black impenetrable swamp. How this section had escaped my observation after some years of constant traveling in the district, I could in no way account for, and I was somewhat piqued to think that a stranger knew more of my own territory than I did myself. More than that, the nature of the whole proposition began to border on the uncanny; even the wild and inhospitable appearance of the landscape, with its grotesque and twisted piles of shattered trees, and dark reaches of brooding swamp, seemed to reflect that atmosphere of weird unreality of this adventure.

The chase was long and I began to tire, and no longer able to run, I now walked; and strangely, I was still able to keep that haunting sound within earshot, and at about the same distance as before. It appeared as if the stranger was cognizant of my fatigue, and was, by some means unknown to me, able to gauge accurately my speed, and thus keep his progress timed to mine, never allowing me to catch up, yet never drawing away from me. And there occurred to me with startling suddenness, the possibility that he did not want to outdistance me, that I had blindly followed where he had led me, and that I had been decoyed with devilish ingenuity many miles into a country of which I knew nothing; for what purpose I could only guess.

The sun had set, and there was no moon; night was coming on and I was alone in a trackless wilderness with an unknown and evidently competent enemy. I became conscious of a feeling of uneasiness, and halting in my tracks, formed and rejected a dozen swift plans of action. Co-incident with my stopping, the sound slewed off to the East beyond a fringe of timber, and I noticed with a feeling of distinct relief that it seemed to be going further away. This, and the fact that I had no provision, decided me to turn back, resolving to return with some supplies and solve this vexing problem on the morrow. Snow threatened, and in that event, the man of mystery must at least leave some tracks.

I squatted on the ice and mapped out as well as I could the tortuous itinerary over which this man-hunt had taken me, in order to devise a short-cut back to my main trail, but found the project hopeless. I was now faced with the necessity of covering the entire route, most of it in the dark.

So I started on the long journey back to my lunching place. Off to one side I could still hear that infernal tock-tock, and as I proceeded I seemed to be unable to get away from the now hateful sound; in fact it seemed to be coming closer. I stopped and listened. It was approaching without a doubt, outflanking me from behind the thin fringe of timber just mentioned, which now proved to be an island behind which it had passed; and a sudden turn in the route brought the sound dead ahead of me, blocking my trail, and coming my way! I could no longer disguise from myself the certainty that this thing, whatever it was, was intentionally heading me off, and mixed with my feeling of affront at the overt act, was more than a hint of fear.

Nearer it came, nearer and yet nearer, and still no one was visible; a slow measured advance, as immutable as the onward march of Time itself; tock, tock, tock; now no longer reminiscent

of the strokes of the homely metronome, but more suggestive of
the ticking of an infernal machine, stalking me, marking off the
seconds till it should close with me and destroy me. In something
of a panic I sheered off, and it followed like a nightmare; I
doubled, and the Thing crept on behind me.

I ran and the sound kept its given distance; I slowed up with
a like result. I twisted, turned, and back-tracked; I tried every
shift and subterfuge learnt in a calling where stratagem and expe-
dient become second nature, but without avail. I could not shake
off my fiendish familiar. And I now knew in cold reality the
awful fear of one pursued by some hellish monster in a nightmare.

I was no longer the pursuer but the pursued, and I was being
hunted by some person or thing that could see without being
seen, and could accurately forestall my every move. Escape into
the bush was impossible, as the whole country was covered by
a fallen forest that had been blown down by some recent hurricane, and in places newly burnt. And always behind and to
one side or the other, that sinister tapping herded me relentlessly
and inexorably on my way, as a steer is herded by a skillful
cowboy. For I dreaded now to meet the one I had so assiduously
sought, and kept as much distance between him and myself as
the shape of the waterways allowed, for I felt that even armed
as I was, weapons would be of little use against a being who
could apparently so flout the laws of nature. I burst into a clammy
sweat.

The terrible hitherto unbelieved tales of the man-eating win-
dego and the Loup Garou, the were-wolf of bush mythology,
flashed across my mind, tales of trappers found dead in ghastly
and unexplainable mutilation.

The horror of what I now knew to be the supernatural drained
the last vestige of resolution from my being, and I abandoned
all attempts at a considered or calculated retreat; I no longer
hoped to outdistance this Thing, seeking only in my desperation
to delay as long as possible the awful moment when it should
catch up to me and work its will upon me.

I lost track of my direction, except to see that I was being
driven deeper and deeper into a savage Wilderness, the like of

which I had never before seen; yet the terror of that unknown presence behind me goaded me on and on, whither, I no longer cared, so that I kept beyond the reach of this invisible peril. I was fatigued beyond measure, and knew that I could not much longer continue my flight. I became obsessed by the idea that if I could only leave the ice I could outdistance my pursuer, but I seemed held from making the attempt by some diabolical power beyond my control.

I then made the alarming discovery that the body of water on which I traveled was coming to an end. Towering, impregnable cliffs walled it in on either hand, closing in on me as the waterway narrowed, and at its termination, no great distance ahead of me, was a bristling rampart of torn and broken tree-trunks, through which no man could made any headway. I now saw that the matter had been brought to an issue, and that be it man, beast, or devil that was hunting me down, I must at last stand and fight it.

My aim was now to reach the foot of the narrow sheet of ice, where I would have protection of a kind on three sides of me, the walls of rock to my flanks, and the masses of fallen timber in my rear. The phantom sound was almost upon me, and not daring to look back lest I lose this terrible race, I stumbled forward with feet that seemed suddenly turned to lead. With a last despairing burst of speed I gained my objective, when hope suddenly sprang to life within me as I descried, by the failing light, a narrow trail that had but lately been hewed through the tangled slash before which I had intended to make my stand. This, I thought, must undoubtedly lead to some human habitation, or failing that, would at least enable me to leave the ice, and so perhaps outdistance my pursuer, whose element it appeared to be, and I made for it with all possilbe speed. My relief at finding my feet on solid ground, where my pursuer would be no longer able to tap out his accursed measure, was indescribable. And then, too late I discovered that a frozen creek ran parallel to the trail, hidden from it by the wall of prostrate tree-trunks, so as to be only intermittently visible. My faulty strategy had now given him the advantage that he needed.

And as, almost at the point of exhaustion, my face streaming with perspiration, and gasping for breath at every step, I staggered along the narrow pathway, the ceaseless tock, tock tock, tock, beat its threat of a nameless horror into my reeling senses, as it marched alongside me on the ice of the stream, an invisible, but ever present escort. I could now no longer turn to right or left, and ever the Thing was beside me; I felt as one who walks with Death.

And then, to my unutterable relief, I saw a clearance ahead of me, and a cluster of log cabins. The stream was now plainly visible, and on its bank a group of men were gathered around some object on the ground, and them I approached with the feelings of one who has escaped from the very edge of the pit. The sound from which I fled was now close at hand, and I lost no time in acquainting those present with my predicament. To my surprise they looked coldly on me, and my remarks passed unheeded. No one spoke, and a strained silence, such as greets the appearance of an unwelcome visitor at any gathering, fell upon the assembly, until one man said, pointing at me:

"There he is now, that is the man; show him his work."

At that the group opened up, and I saw stretched out before me the dead body of a young man, terribly mutilated, evidently murdered with the utmost brutality.

"Who has done this?" I asked, even as there was borne upon me the frightful realization that these people, for some reason, accounted me the guilty party. My question remained unanswered, but all eyes were turned on me with cold, staring hostility. These men were all rough prospectors and trappers, strangers to me, every one of them, members of a community that I had not known even existed, and their deadly calm and purposeful demeanour showed me that the situation was fraught with terrible possibilities.

I made some attempt to clear myself, telling them who I was, and where I had been this two months past, stumbling over my words and faltering in my speech, as an innocent man will, when confronted by the evidence of his supposed guilt.

My disjointed and incoherent protestations met with no response; the men ignored the fact that I was speaking, staring at me in stony silence, on their faces the set expression of an unalterable purpose. Finally the man who had accused me spoke again. "This thing must be finished before dark. Here comes the boy's father; let him decide what is to be done." And at that instant the persistent, unearthly rapping that had driven me to the scene of what was liable to be my doom, at length caught up to me and, almost at my elbow, abruptly ceased. Turning, I now for the first time saw my pursuer, an old, old man dressed in faded buckskin, and armed with a heavy, steel-shod hardwood pole. His frame was so attenuated, being almost fleshless, and his demeanour so strange and wild, that he had all the semblance of one risen from the grave, or of a being from another world. His hair was white and hung in snaky locks below his shoulders, and a full beard covered most of his face; and out of this his burning eyes glared into mine with an unwavering stare of such malevolence and hatred, that it chilled me to the bone; for I plainly saw what he would desire to be done.

Without speaking he advanced on me slowly, raising above his head as he did so the heavy staff that, having driven me to my place of execution, was now to be the instrument of his just but misdirected vengeance.

The first blow struck by the parent as his unalienable right, I would then, without a shadow of doubt, be literally shot to pieces. Stiff with horror, held by some awful fascination in the old man's insane stare, I was struck dumb, until at last:

"Wait, men, wait." I screeched rather than shouted "I am not the man," fumbling meanwhile in my pockets with fingers that refused their office, for some identification. Two men leaped forward quickly, and held me full in the path of the descending shaft. In my dire extremity and with the strength of despair, I tore myself loose with a mighty effort. A great light flashed before my eyes, and I awoke to find the landlord of the little frontier hotel, where I was passing the night, shaking me violently with one hand, while he held a lamp before my face with the other.

And at the same moment there came to my ears the steady and resonant ticking of the large kitchen clock that was suspended on the wall over my bed.

STORY OUTLINE

I. Grey Owl is in his cabin and hears the steady tock, tock, tock, of a man coming closer, testing the ice on the lake as he comes.

II. In the tradition of the north country, he prepares a warmer fire and fixes tea and something to eat for his arriving visitor.

III. He is shocked to realize that the man has passed by the cabin. This is an insult in the north country -- he rushes out to chase the man down and find out who he is.

IV. For over an hour he follows the man, thinking to easily overcome his slow pace. The sound swings to the right down a deep bay, unfamiliar to Grey Owl.

V. For hours he continues, following the steady tap, tap, tap -- through gorges, over wide expanses of lakes, along forest bordered streams, but always on ice listening to the tap, tap, tap.

VI. It soon begins to get dark, and Grey Owl is becoming fatigued. He notices that the tapping has slowed, as if the man knows he is tiring. He decides that he is almost lost in unknown territory at night, with an unknown enemy ahead of him. His best plan would be to return. The tapping man has gone into the forest and the sound is fading.

VII. As Grey Owl starts his trip back, he finds that the tapping man has simply gone around an island and is now heading straight for him!

VIII. Grey Owl shears off to one side. The tock, tock, tock of the tapping is louder and following him, like a monstrous machine closing to destroy him. If he ran, slowed, changed course, it followed.

IX. He realizes that the lake he is on came to a dead end with cliffs blocking his retreat. He decides to make a stand in a protected bay, but upon reaching it is delighted to find a new trail recently cut into the wilderness.

X. Hoping to find humans, he takes the trail. The tapping follows him as there is a stream running along side of the trail. On this narrow trail, he can turn neither right nor left to escape from the tapping monster that is right beside him.

XI. To his relief a clearing is ahead with several men standing beside the now visible river. The tapping is right behind him. He approaches the men, only to see a crumpled figure lying at their feet.

XII. One of the men points to him, saying: ''There he is now, that is the man; show him his work.'' At their feet lays the terribly mutilated body of a young man, apparently murdered.

XIII. The men pay no attention to Grey Owl's telling them he was innocent. They state that here comes the boy's father now, let him decide what should be done.

XIV. Grey Owl is horrified to hear the tapping resounding behind him ever louder; turning it is the boy's father, a wild looking man, who looms closer and closer with a fierce stare of hatred. The old man approaches Grey Owl and raises the heavy, metal tipped staff he has been using to strike the ice, raises it to smash it down on Grey Owl's head.

XV. Grey Owl pleads with the men, who are holding him for the old man to strike. Grey Owl struggles and struggles -- suddenly he finds himself being shaken awake by the landlord of the little frontier hotel where he has fallen asleep, with their large kitchen clock ticking loudly on the wall suspended over his bed.

What a nightmare! When telling this story use plenty of tap, tap, tap and tock, tock, tocks to describe the incessant noise of the ice walker Grey Owl is encountering. Using the descriptive phrases that Grey Owl includes of his journey through the icy wilderness makes this a great, scary campfire story.

THE MESSAGE

as told by Doc Forgey

At Fort Bragg, North Carolina, the father of one of my scouts got himself into trouble. This is an area that has a lot of nice sandy soil, beautiful pine trees -- it is also an area of swamps. And, in those swamps, one has to be careful and remain alert as to what he is doing. You should not become too mesmerized by walking and day dreaming, by enjoying a walk in the woods without maintaining at least a certain amount of vigilance.

This particular hunter was very smart because when he left for a pheasant hunt he told people where he was going and when he would be returning. He went alone, which always increases the risk one might run when traveling in the swamps, but at least he notified others of his planned whereabouts.

A long day hiking in the hot, North Carolina sun tends to exhaust a person. Enjoying the beautiful countryside at the same time also lulls one into a comfortable, mechanical stride that minimizes the effort. He was walking along, paying no attention to where he was going. As he was moving, he failed to notice that he was entering a depression, a shallow valley-like area. Suddenly, something moved catching his eye and jarring him to reality!

What moved? To his astonishment it was a snake at his feet, but not just a snake slithering away from him, but a sudden excitement and rippling movement of dozens of snakes, all Eastern diamondback rattlesnakes, lying virtually on top of each other, spread all throughout the depression area and surrounding him on all sides!

Reacting with instinct, he gave a leap upon a stump that was moldering in the ground next to him. He stared in horror at the writhing mass of snakes, all deadly poisonous and now all awake and active -- crawling over each other, hissing, and even striking at each other. The heat in this depressed area was oppressive. But fear more than the heat made the sweat stream down his face. He had his .410 shotgun with him, but he knew that he did not have enough shells to clear his way through this mass of snakes.

As he stood there staring in fascination looking all about him, the movement of the snakes gradually quieted down. They again became dormant -- fewer and fewer of them seemed to have noticed the intrusion upon their resting place. He could not believe what had happened. His heart was still pounding at the thought of his narrow escape and with apprehension about his present situation. He could not understand how he walked into the middle of this mess without being bitten! But now here he was -- stuck in the middle of a swampy depression, surrounded by poisonous snakes, any one of which could possibly kill him, or at least cause terrible injury.

At least they were not attempting to climb up the stump to get him. But if noise and excitement seemed to have left this valley, the heat had not. Standing there on the stump, the heat seemed more and more oppressive. Afraid to move a muscle for fear of arousing the snakes, the hunter wisely stood as motionless as possible. He hoped that the snakes would leave this area when the day cooled down towards evening. Perhaps then he could find a pathway out of this mess.

The minutes passed like hours, slowly -- almost imperceptibly. The heat and sweating added to the thirst of his earlier activity. His mouth was parched, his legs fatigued. His only hope was that these snakes would leave the valley after it cooled. Perhaps they would become fearful of owls or other creatures of the night -- if only he could just remain perched where he was until night fall.

Perching on a stump is never easy. In this case it was sheer torture. It seemed as if the sun would never lower, that the day would never cool.

SUDDENLY, a clatter and hissing snapped him awake! His shotgun had fallen from his sweaty grasp! While this commotion continued for a few minutes, the heat of the afternoon soon caused it to slow down. Soon the only sound was the occasional buzz of a fly, the occasional slither or hiss of a restless snake.

But finally, the imperceptible movement of the sun, lower and lower towards the horizon, did make a difference. It became cooler and more tolerable, but this dimming of the sun's rays caused a stir throughout the depression. The snakes were becoming more active, they were moving in anticipation of feeding -- more at ease in the cooler evening temperatures!

The hunter stared in horror as the snakes raised their heads, hissing at each other. His skin crawled whenever some of the nearby snakes seemed to notice the stump, when their actions seemed to indicate an interest in his position. His escape at night now seemed in doubt.

Darkness finally came. He had stood on that stump as long as he possibly could. He was dehydrated. He was exhausted. The snakes were still twined all around the stump and escape had become impossible. There was no moon. The stars seemed distant and unfriendly. If he stared at one too long, it seemed to move -- almost as if it wanted to pull him off that stump!

And that stump. His feet were now made sore by every lump and irregularity on it. The pain did not stop at his feet. It traveled up his legs making every muscle in his body ache.

AAAUUUGGGHHH!

A shout, a scream broke the silence of the night! The noise startled him awake -- almost startled him off the log. *(If the above is handled properly, when you scream, everyone at the campfire will think that he has fallen off the log, hence the scream!)*. Bright lights shined in his face, making it impossible to see in the surrounding darkness!

With a startle he realized that his wait was over -- a whole group of rescuers had found him, had shouted to him and turned their lights upon him. Calling encouragement to him, they carefully started shooting the snakes that were crawling near their position or along the pathway they had chosen to reach the stump. He was saved -- saved because he had left a message where he could be found!

STORY OUTLINE

I. A hunter decided to leave for a walk in the woods of North Carolina looking for pheasant. He went alone, but he left a message telling his family where he would be going and when he would be returning.

II. The hunter became entranced with the beauty of the walk, paying no attention to where he was going. Suddenly a movement caught his eye -- it was a snake, in fact he had wandered into a depression full of snakes!

III. He jumped upon a nearby stump, watching in horror as the snakes crawled, hissing around him.

IV. The day slowly passed, the hot sun, the aching of his legs, the drone of an occasional fly -- suddenly a clatter and hissing snapped him awake. His shotgun had fallen from his sweaty grasp.

V. The snakes quieted down until the setting sun allowed the valley to cool. This seemed to cause the snakes to become more active. Escape seemed impossible.

VI. Darkness came. He was exhausted. The ache

in his body traveled up his legs into every muscle in his body.

VII. AAAUUUGGGHHH! A loud scream broke the silence of the night. The noise startled him awake. He realized that the lights and noise were the rescuers, that his wait was over.

VIII. He was saved -- saved because he had left a message where he could be found!

THE HAUNTING OF THE HOUSE ON THE RIDGE

as told by Doc Forgey

They say that the house is haunted. I don't know if it is really haunted or not, but a terrible tragedy happened there. The kind that one could imagine would cause a haunting.

It is a small house, but it has 2 stories. It is located on a ridge in Brown County in Southern Indiana. It was an area where many people lived at one time on small farms. Farms so small that they eventually had to be abandoned -- the families moving to the city to make a living. The narrow valleys where the early pioneers had settled could barely allow the cultivation of a few fields, adequate only for subsistence until the gradual inflation of prices finally made even that impossible.

Up until the 1920's these small homesteads were still used by families. The area was wild enough that they could add to their food supply by hunting in the woods for rabbit, squirrels and deer. There was even a natural salt lick nearby where the earliest pioneers could even mine the salt that they needed. Now abandoned, up on a ridge behind Camp Palawopec, there stands such a homestead. It is a decaying, two story house. One wonders why such a well built house would have been abandoned -- why this property was not taken over and lived in again?

There was once a family that lived there. The father worked their property in the valley, growing crops for their meager cash needs and for food. Mom was kept busy with her chores of canning, picking berries, keeping the house, and the endless chores that go with living a primitive country existence. Their son was old enough to help his dad in the fields, but the thing that he liked to do most was to hunt in the nearby ridges for squirrels, rabbits, and what other game he could find. This was an important source of food for the family and he was proud of how well he could hunt.

During the winter months he was forced -- like so many other youngsters -- to go to school, which meant he had to hunt during the very brief time between getting home and dark. His mom and dad would always wait supper for him, giving him a chance to range out to one of the better hunting spots. Because of this they would often eat supper after dark.

One fine autumn day he took off squirrel hunting. That evening, when darkness fell, his family waited for him as usual. But this night the wait was longer than usual -- for it got later and later, yet he did not return!

At first his family was not in the least worried. But as the hours passed after darkness, they became very concerned. He always returned shortly after dark as he was as hungry as they were.

Walking in the forest at night was not easy. Perhaps he had strayed too far and was having a hard time getting back. His mother lit several lanterns and placed them on both trails leading towards the house. His father set out on foot in the last direction that they had seem him take. When his father finally returned it was about 10:00 p.m. -- his mother was very worried.

His dad saddled the horse and rode to the nearby town of Nashville, Indiana. There he went to the sheriff's home and told him his son was missing in the woods and they were worried about him. The sheriff called his force together and they also alerted the volunteer fire department, all of whom proceeded to the homestead.

That night they accomplished nothing except to realize the boy was very lost, or badly hurt out of ear-shot from any of the trails that they had searched in the night. Early the next morning the rescue crews assembled at the homestead and planned the course of action. They would have to divide up the entire surrounding area so that they could search every valley, every hill trail that he might have wandered away from. He might have tripped and knocked himself out, or shot himself, so they were anxious to find him as soon as possible.

Several of the wives from town gathered at the homestead also. They brought food to help feed the search and rescue parties. A tent was set up in front of the house in which to feed the crews and shelter them in case of rain as they came and went. They worked all day and into the night. The next day they were still working at it, with a few more people arriving from town.

The rescuers worked frantically, making trip after trip along the woodland trails in this hilly, and densely covered region of Indiana. As the third day approached, his disappearance was still a mystery and the situation seemed even more desperate.

It was on this third day that something unusual occurred. The ladies working in the kitchen began to notice that the water was acquiring a strange taste! Most houses built on a ridge made use of a water cistern for the water supply. A cistern is a well used to collect rain water from the roof. In the case of this house the cistern was located just behind the house and the water lifted out of the hole by a bucket. One of the ladies mentioned this to the boy's father, who decided he would check into it...

He lifted the cover near the cistern opening to let sunlight shine in, and peered down. There, to his horror, was the body of his son -- bloated and floating at the top of the well! He had accidentally fallen into the cistern and drowned! Unable to climb back out, he must have hung on for hours, finally his strength failing him, he slid under the water to his death.

Never was a family so grief-stricken as they were. The boy's body was recovered and the rescue party quickly left. Soon after the family decided that they could no longer live there. The house was deserted and remains so to this day. It was because of cases like this that people have always been warned to cover wells and abandoned shafts.

It was this terrible tragedy that caused a particular house to be left to ruin on a ridge in southern Indiana. Even to this day when I visit there I can sense the immense pain and suffering that surrounds the old house. One can stand by the covered cistern and even go up the old stairs to the boy's bedroom. If one dares to do so, alone, at night, it is said that a cold musty smell will appear from nowhere. And many who have been there have actually heard their name called out. Any place that has seen a tragedy seems to acquire a mysterious sadness -- but no place that I have seen compares with the intense loneliness of this place. Almost as if the boy's ghost in the cistern is calling out for companionship.

STORY OUTLINE

I. The son of a homestead family leaves on his evening chore of hunting for the family table.

II. When he does not return for dinner, his family searches for him, then sends for the sheriff.

III. Search parties are based at the house and for the next three days comb the woods looking for him.

IV. On the third day several of the women cooking for the search party notice a strange taste to the cistern water.

V. The father opens the cistern lid, looking inside he discovers the body of his son, who must have fallen in and drowned rather than having gone hunting as was originally guessed.

VI. The family cannot live there after this terrible tragedy. They abandon their homestead forever.

VII. The loneliness of this place is evident even to this day -- and at night one feels the boy's presence when visiting the house.

THE CURSE OF THE AUSTRALIAN GOLD

as told by Doc Forgey

Introduction

It is hard to discount or ignore tales told by well established important men in their community who insist that they have been cursed; that ghosts have contacted them. These men cannot be dismissed lightly. Such a tale was told by George Woodfall. He was a wealthy man from Sidney, Australia. This is the strange, supposedly true, story of a curse and ghosts that haunted him in the middle of the last century.

* * * * *

George Woodfall was originally from England. He was from a well respected family, but he lost all of his money in business dealings causing him to immigrate to Australia to seek his fortune. And what better way to seek one's fortune in the outback than prospecting for gold?

He found two partners, Harper and Freeth, and together they searched the back country of Australia for gold. Woodfall was hoping to find enough that he could rebuild his fortune. Harper and Freeth were typical prospectors -- two rough characters looking for an easy strike so that they could live it up awhile in town before heading out again to look for more gold.

They were lucky, little by little they found gold. The nuggets and specks kept adding up until they were happy with their find -- at least Harper and Freeth were. They were slowly working their way back to Sidney, Australia, to spend their fortunes when they noticed a remarkable waterfall leaping out of the side of a cliff. Such a remarkable sight was made even more appealing for the mountain slope contained considerable quartz, which is frequently a gold bearing rock. Even from the ground they could see a cave entrance near the waterfall. Certainly they should look into such a find!

They crawled up the rubble slope to the cave entrance. Once there they found that the cave entrance was a vertical shaft straight down. Chopping up some sturdy small trees, they fashioned pegs which they could drive in cracks in the rock, thus making a ladder that they could climb down. In this manner they were able to make it to the bottom of this cave. It was very impressive, with a vast cathedral like ceiling which reverberated to the thunderous roar of the nearby waterfall. Large stalagtites and stalagmites[1] glittered in their torch light. Beautiful quartz crystals in the walls reflected their light. Excited by the possibility of a rich find, they set to work, digging into the quartz veins in the walls, heedless of the extreme beauty that surrounded them.

But beauty was all that they would find, for the quartz had very little evidence of gold in it. At one point they smashed a large quartz formation, finding a small den of a cave behind it. Exhausted by their work, they decided to rest in the small den before climbing out and proceeding on their way to Sidney. They were able to gather firewood from the shattered trees that had fallen down the shaft. In the warmer confines of the den, they lit their fire and settled down for the night.

Their talk that night, as usual, was of their gold, calculating its worth and describing the meals they would eat and the fun

---

[1] Stalagtites are the rock formations that hang down from the ceilings of caves, while stalagmites grow from the ground up.

they would have when they reached Sidney. But Woodfall fell into a silent brooding since he was an impatient man. Each had a respectable amount of gold, but these men he was with had little ambition. The gold they had would soon be squandered. If he could only have the entire amount, then he would be wealthy enough to really make a come-back!

There would be no chance of simply robbing his two companions and running to Sidney or anywhere else with the gold. They would follow him to the ends of the earth. As he pondered the situation, he eventually came to a bone chilling plan. He would murder his companions. But they were both strong men, both clever desert travelers. He would have to be swift and sure of himself.

The fire was dying down -- he would need light, but just enough light to accomplish his task. Not so much light that they might notice his movements. How would he kill both of these men almost at once? Would they never stop talking, laughing, carrying on? He took some of the breakfast fire wood and added a little to the fire. Neither man seemed to pay attention to him. And soon, fortunately, they seemed to fall asleep. He waited until he could hear the even, deep breathing one expects in sleeping men.

His plans well laid, he waited until the fire died -- he could barely see Freeth, his closest victim. He would have to dispatch him and instantly roll to Harper's position and hit him anywhere he could. Sweat was standing on his brow, even in the cool damp cave. His muscles tense, he knew the time was right -- it was now or never.

Quick as a flash, he struck Freeth a death blow right to the heart! There was scarcely a gurgle, simply a convulsion as the man received this lethal blow. Then he flung himself towards Harper. Woodfall had failed to count on the almost sixth sense that a woodsman develops to danger -- that sixth sense had caused Harper to spring awake. Harper had turned to grab for his pistol as Woodfall lunged at him. Woodfall tackled him -- both the knife and gun clattered away onto the darkness of the cave floor. Woodfall had the advantage as he grabbed Harper around the throat and squeezed like a mad man. Harper had been unable to get a breath of air and thus soon thrashed, tangled in his bed roll as he convulsed from the lack of oxygen. Woodfall let the unconscious man loose, but searched for his knife. Locating it by its glitter in the dim light, he instantly turned back towards the strangled Harper. Harper was sitting, unable to speak as he was still gasping for breath, but his pitiful face could be seen, his face flushed, his eyes protruding. He looked up at Woodfall desperately, putting his hands together, praying for mercy. But Woodfall had gone too far to stop now. He plunged the knife straight into Harper's chest.

AAAUUUGGGHHH!

Harper died with a terrible scream that echoed and reverberated through the great room of the nearby large cave.

Even though it was the middle of the night, Woodfall decided to leave that place at once. He combined the gold which they had all mined into his pack. The twisted bodies of his companions were too much for his conscience, and he decided to bury them. Perhaps he could hide any evidence of his crime forever in the bottom of the small grotto.

But digging in that cave bottom was harder work than he thought. The floor was clay, packed hard as concrete, with many small rocks. He chiseled away at it, but tiring he decided just to lay them in the shallow grave he had constructed and lay what debris he had picked from the floor over them. There would be little chance anyone would find this remote location, and if they did, there was nothing that could connect him with their deaths anyway.

Thus he left them, partially covered with loose rubble. He attached a rope to his now heavy saddle bags, then carefully climbed up the treacherous wooden stakes they had placed in the entrance shaft. He left this horror behind him for Sidney, where his fortune awaited him. The date was September 20th -- a day that would soon mean a lot to George Woodfall.

Once there he established himself as a wealthy man from England, who was interested in investing his money in various Australian enterprises. Woodfall was obviously a man who took

chances. When the opportunity arose, he invested nearly everything in a new mining property called the Benambra Mine, soon
to become one the wealthiest mines in Australia. The shares
skyrocketed and he found himself a very rich man.

He purchased an estate in an exclusive area of Sidney called
Pott's Point. There he lived in a grand style. He entertained
lavishly and soon had many friends in the highest levels of society.
But soon September came around. After one party he sat alone
by an open window in his sitting room, staring across the dark
waters of Port Jackson to the harbor lights at the Heads. More
and more his conscience ate at him -- he would have given back
all of his wealth, if only the terrible deed which he had done
could be reversed. In this frame of mind, he had a strong incli-
nation to go to the police and confess his crime. Soon this mood
passed. He sank back into his chair thinking that at least dead
men could tell no tales, and those men were hardly fit to have
owned that wealth which they would have merely lost within a
month.

Suddenly, he heard a voice in the room say, "It is time.
Let us begin."

Sure that he had overheard burglars, he slipped to his desk
and obtained a revolver. He searched the house, but was unable
to find any evidence of intruders. He returned the revolver to his
desk. Deciding to go to bed, he put out the lights in the room
and started for the door. He had hardly taken a step, when he
said that he heard a heavy thump, like a body falling at his feet.
As he staggered back in alarm, he began to hear sounds -- the
sound of a waterfall reverberating in the room, then worst of all
came an ear piercing scream, just like the last terrible cry made
by Harper when Woodfall plunged the knife into his chest. There
were other terrible, unknown noises which shook and rebounded
through the room.

He collapsed into a corner, covering his ears against the
terrible bedlam, but he was unable to drown this living nightmare
out. It was as if he was back in the cave, reliving that night of
terror -- the night he sent two of his companions to the next world.

He expected his servants to hear this racket and come flying down from their quarters. But no one came and he soon guessed that only he could hear this nightmare of sounds -- the devil's concert as he later called it.

At the height of this noise it suddenly ceased. Then, next to him a voice spoke, plain as day. It was the voice of the slain Harper.

"You are growing forgetful, George. In a week's time it will be September the twentieth. We are here to remind you."

George Woodfall remembered the voice -- without doubt it was Harper's, whose nightmarish scream had haunted him so long. But he also felt, rather than heard, another presence. That of Freeth whom he had killed so suddenly.

"Your time has not come yet, George, but before it does we will teach you to remember. We will expect you in the cave on the twentieth. Don't forget to come. That is the only way you will escape us."

"Yes, I will come," Woodfall answered, and then he fell into a dream.

Was it a visit from beyond, or merely the tortured mind of a man who had committed cold blooded murder?

Nevertheless, Woodfall returned to the cave, fearful of disobeying the dreaded specter who had contacted him beyond the grave. The trip back had to be made alone and in secret. Once there he had to again thrust in the wooden pegs to support his weight as he climbed down into that chamber of horrors. Woodfall later said of his experience that there he spent "a night of such agonizing horror that I wondered afterwards how I came to retain either life or reason."

What actually took place in the cave that night? We can only guess, but it would be doubtful that Woodfall could have touched the decaying bodies of his victims, covered with the thin layer of rocks.

Each year after this he repeated his ghastly journey, spending a whole night in this hellish pit -- listening to the roar of the waterfall. Each year the bodies rotted more and more, becoming more skeletal, more decayed. It was only by going back there that he felt he could have peace between times. But each year his dread of September twentieth mounted.

During the fourth year he decided that he would not go. But there was to be no escape, for again Harper and Freeth visited him at Pott's Point, turning his home into a raging hell. From that time on, he never tried, never hoped to avoid the yearly pilgrimage to this cave of death.

This grim yearly ritual had one major effect upon George Woodfall. It changed his whole attitude towards life. No more did he hold frivolous parties. He tried to make up for his deed by giving to charity. He went to church regularly. He became one of Sidney's most respected citizens. His importance to the community is the reason that we are so aware of what eventually happened to him.

No one could possibly have guessed that he was a murderer. He had kept his gruesome secret well. Even his yearly trips had been carefully planned so that no one followed him, or even missed him. But the urge to confess his deed was constantly beneath the surface. Perhaps Harper and Freeth would leave him in peace if he confessed to the authorities? Anything would be better than the visit to the dreaded cave.

Finally, after twenty wretched years, and after nineteen terrifying visits to the cave of horror, Woodfall decided that he would make a complete confession. He felt compelled to make one more pilgrimage. But before he left, he sat down and wrote out his confession, noting the details of the murders, his many trips to the cave in penance, but particularly the visits of the ghosts of Harper and Freeth to his home at Pott's Point. He then left his home, never to return. His disappearance was a sensation in Sidney. All of his property and business dealings were found to be in perfect order. A statue was erected to the memory of this great civic leader. But, his disappearance was also a mystery that would not be solved for five years.

The mystery was solved by William Rowley, the architect of many canals in New South Wales, and the Reverend Charles Power, of St. Chrysostom Church, Redfern, Sydney. They went on an expedition into the wilds of the Blue Mountains, gathering specimens for Rev. Power's large collection of butterflies. Both of them had known George Woodfall personally.

It was the twentieth of September when they came upon the spectacular waterfall which had first attracted Woodfall, Freeth, and Harper nearly 25 years before. They camped near the base of the waterfall, delighted with the beauty of the area. Just after supper, while relaxing around the campfire, a thunderstorm rolled around them. A deep red glare shone through the clouds which seemed to turn the pouring torrent of water to a crimson, blood color. This caused them to stare closely at the waterfall and in so doing they noticed the figure of a man -- rather the image of a man along the edge of the waterfall. The image seemed to be beckoning them up the slope.

Although it was dark and treacherous, they scrambled up the hill. It took them an hour and a half to reach the place where they saw the man. They were following a dim trail along a steep precipice, with the mountain towering above them steeply in the night. In another hour they had reached the summit where the waterfall leaped off into the valley below. There they noted an ironbark tree which had been blazed with an arrow pointing directly downwards.

In the nearby brush they found the entrance of the cave shaft. They held their lantern over the black pit and noted the wooden pegs which had been driven in the shaft wall. The stakes seemed secure, so the two men daringly descended. After a struggle with the treacherous entrance shaft, they found themselves at the bottom of the main cave, standing in awe at its size, listening to the roar of the cascading falls nearby. They examined the magnificent chunks of broken quartz, the beautiful cave formations, and the large boulders that littered the cavern floor.

Finally Rowley found the entrance of the smaller cave and entered it! His cry of horror brought Revered Power hurrying in after him. As Power joined him, Rowley said, ''Come, let's go back. This is no place for us!''

''For heaven's sake, what is it?'' Power demanded.

Rowley then turned the full effect of his lantern upon the scene in the grotto. There in front of them was the shallow open grave, the tools used to dig it still scattered about, but sitting on the edge of the grave was a skeleton, bush clothes rotted to tatters, sitting as if he was peering, grinning down into the grave.

Two more bodies lay in the grave, one on top of the other. The one on top was similarly an almost complete decomposed skeleton. The one underneath was not as decayed as the other two!

Rowley reached down with a sapling and brushed aside the top corpse to view the one beneath. He was in the last stages of decay, but the dried flesh on the face made him seem vaguely familiar. There was something obviously strange about positioning of the bodies. Why was one less decomposed than the others on the bottom? The other two had obviously been dead a much longer time. How was it possible for the man who had died last to be found underneath a man who had died many years before?

They noted some camping gear and searched through it. In an old coat, fallen apart from age and the dampness of the cave, they found a flat metal box containing the inscription: "George Woodfall, Pott's Point, Sidney." Within that box they had the answer of the mystery which they were staring at, or at least a part of the mystery. Inside was the confession of George Woodfall, how he had killed Harper and Freeth for their gold, and how they had made him return to this place every year.

In his confession he wrote that he was making this, his twentieth trip, his last trip. He planned to return to the authorities and turn his confession over to them. He would never again return to this horrid cave.

But he did not return from his twentieth trip. He did not leave the power of Harper and Freeth ever again. How was he killed?

He had originally laid the bodies of his two victims in the grave which he had dug. And there they had laid during the twenty years of his visits, slowly decomposing. Because of his fear and loathing of this horrid place, it is hard to imagine him in anyway disturbing or touching their bodies.

But he said that this would be his last visit to this place -- from this point on he would attempt to free himself from the power of the dead. And to help him do it he would give himself up to the authorities, to be locked in prison so that he could NOT return, even if he wanted to try. Perhaps the ghosts of Freeth and Harper which had such great power over him prevented his ever leaving again. Perhaps he arrived to find them sitting on the edge of the grave awaiting his return? Or perhaps he went hopelessly insane during this, his last visit to the cave.

The Reverend Charles Power felt that there was something very devilish about the whole thing -- that the place smelt like the very pit of hell.

The two men buried the three bodies, the Reverend Power saying a prayer over them. A cairn was constructed outside the entrance of the grotto marking their grave site -- a cairn made of beautiful gold-bearing crystalline quartz from the cavern floor.

STORY OUTLINE

I. George Woodfall murders two companions in a cave located near a waterfall, high on a cliff, to steal their gold. Freeth he kills instantly, Harper struggles but is finally half strangled and then stabbed to death.

II. Woodfall invests his money well and becomes a very wealthy and respected man in Sidney, Australia. But he is haunted on the anniversary of the murder -- voices in his house and the sound of the waterfall convince him to return to the scene of his crime.

III. He returns yearly, spending the night in the cave with the bodies of his victims, during the next 19 years.

IV. Finally, he decides he will return only one last time and afterwards make a confession to the police.

He never returns from this secret trip to the cave.

V. Five years later two men stumble across the waterfall. They notice the appearance image of a man who seems to beckon them up the hill, where they find the cave.

VI. Inside they find the bodies of three men. Two have been dead a long time. Two men are in the shallow grave dug by Woodfall -- and he is one of them! One of the older corpses is located on top of him, the other is sitting on the side of the grave. They find Woodfall's confession, thus learning the whole incredible story, which was recorded in the Sidney newspapers.

THE LOST HUNTER

as told by Doc Forgey

The Adirondacks has many beautiful places to camp. It is an old, and in many places a wild area. There have been many stories that have come from the Adirondack Mountains. This particular story, told in the Pennsylvania region, is a story of a lost hunter.

One weekend a group of guys went hunting, back into the remote hills of the Adirondacks. In that country there are plenty of deer and they all hoped one of them would be lucky enough to get one for their families. It was a very cold day, one threatening to snow. They had permission to use a cabin from its owner, so they felt they would be safe in case of a storm.

At about the time that they arrived at the cabin, a very light snow had, indeed, already begun to fall. The one essential thing was to be able to keep warm in that cabin. They opened the door and found that everything was intact, no damage had been done. The cabin had a nice Franklin stove to one side of the room which looked sturdy and which should maintain a good, warm glow throughout the night.

There was one problem which they now discovered. There was no firewood where the wood pile should have been located. The previous occupant of the building had failed to cut firewood and replace what he had burned. There was not a stick to be found. Obviously they were going to have to get out in the few remaining moments of day light and gather some wood real fast. Darkness was coming as well as the possibility of an approaching storm. With snow clouds formed overhead, darkness would indeed come early.

They scattered out around the cabin, each man trying to find some wood. If a cabin has been built for any length of time, generally it means that all of the readily available wood suitable for burning in that area has been used. All of the easily gathered wood has been picked up or pulled off of trees already. One has to then go further and further away to get a firewood supply. And that was just the case for these men. There was no wood that they could use right near the cabin and they had to spread out further and further to find the wood that they so desperately needed.

There was one man, John Butler, who did wander and wander. He strayed down into a little valley ravine where he hoped to find downed squaw wood to burn. The tricky part about wandering in an area which is cut up into ravines, ridges, and valleys is that you may feel you know where you are, but by climbing over a ridge into a wrong ravine you can easily be lead into a maze of wrong ridges and your directions can easily become very twisted and confusing. You can end up not heading in the direction that you thought you were going. This, indeed, proved to be the fate of John Butler. For on this cold, stormy evening he disappeared into the night.

The snow was cascading down worse and worse. The darkness settled in, which combined with the swirling snow, made visibility virtually zero. His friends returned back to the cabin fairly soon for they realized how dangerous it was to be out at night in a snow storm, especially in territory that they really weren't familiar with. But John Butler had been caught, extending himself out too far, and was trapped in a swirling snow storm in the Adirondacks in Pennsylvania.

His friends were really quite concerned about him. They waited impatiently for him to appear. When he didn't return after about 2 hours, they felt they would have to get out there and look for him. It would take too long to get into town, the road may not be passable, and his tracks would certainly disappear if they waited much longer. The temperature was dropping and John could be getting into trouble, maybe he was even injured!

They took the lanterns that they had brought and placed kerosene lights in the cabin's two windows. They tried to follow what they thought might be his trail, each person trying to determine who had made the marks that they were following, trying to determine if they were following the trail of the lost hunter.

It became quite apparent after struggling in a fiercer and fiercer blizzard that it would be absolutely impossible to find him that night. The trails were becoming rapidly obscured. The weather was so bad, that the best they could do was to return to the cabin and try to survive the storm themselves. They had only found a few scraps of wood, so they didn't have a very pleasant night of it. But huddled there together, listening to the gale winds tearing at the cabin and the trees groaning outside, they feared for their friend's life.

When morning came, the snow continued. Two of the men took their 4-wheel drive vehicle and drove into town to get the sheriff who alerted the local Search and Rescue team. The rescue team soon congregated at the cabin site deep in the woods. They had brought their tracking dogs, food, clothing, and heaters to establish a base camp for the search operation.

They struck out looking for him. The dogs proved useless in the confusion of tracks and the blowing snow drifts. The search drug on for days. Ridges were combed, valleys and ravines were checked. They gave up all hope of finding him alive. Indeed, when a person is lost in a driving snow storm, frequently their body will be covered so well that it might not be found until after the Spring thaw.

But the story of John Butler does not end there. While this area is very remote, it is still active with camping and hiking. A scout camp was located only thirty miles away and the Appalachian trail passes through a neighboring section of land. The next fall a group of scouts reported an unusual occurrence.

Members of Troop 91 from Colfield had left the scout camp

3 days before on a fifty mile hike. The evening of their third day, three members of the troop were sleeping somewhat apart from the others, but near the cooking fire embers left over from supper. Harold Johnson, a Patrol Leader, was asleep in the area that had been the wood pile. Had been, I said, because all of the fire wood had been consumed cooking supper and for general warmth and campfire fun afterward. After hiking all day one tends to be tired, very tired. Yet, in the middle of the night John sensed something wrong and he just popped awake...

And he wished that he hadn't!

Standing next to him he saw a man, and the man was holding an axe! In fact, it appeared to be his troop's axe. John broke out in a cold sweat, his eyes barely open, peeking at what the man was going to do next.

Suddenly the man moved, WHAM! QUICK AS A FLASH THE AXE SLAMMED INTO THE TREE NEAR HIS HEAD!

John opened his eyes wide in terror ... but the man was gone!

He bolted up out of his sleeping bag, paying no attention to the night's chill. He virtually landed on his two friends nearby, shaking them awake, telling them what he had seen. They fumbled for their flashlights and shined them around looking for any trace of the man John had just seen.

They did not see the man, but what they did see was a stack of firewood, left where they had laid their axe that night! Needless to say, the entire troop was awake within about 3 minutes with the guys looking for clues of this missing man. He vanished without a trace, no foot prints, nothing. Nothing but the stack of firewood and their axe stuck in the tree.

As the years went on, the stories of encounters with the Lost Hunter kept spreading out. The sightings started happening further and further away from the lonely cabin. People in nearby states started telling a story of a mysterious man visiting their campsite, of their finding firewood where none had been the night before.

It seemed that the ghost of this lost hunter was prowling around, just waiting, looking to find somebody who was impolite enough not to chop firewood to leave for people who might come afterwards, or perhaps lazy enough not to chop enough to have some there for emergencies -- or for people who had burned all of theirs up and did not have any left in case the weather became bad or some problem developed. It became real important to everyone in that area to remember one of the basic courtesies and rules of camping -- to plan ahead, to make sure that there was firewood available and to make sure that the campsite was left in better shape than when they first found it.

If you are out camping and the weather is bad, particularly as a snow storm swirls in, be sure that you have plenty of firewood, both for yourself or for others that might follow you. Campers who do not obtain enough firewood are apt to have a visit in the middle of the night from the Lost Hunter!

STORY OUTLINE

I. A group of hunters travel deep into the Adirondack Mountains to a cabin they have borrowed for a weekend of deer hunting.

II. When they get there a snow storm begins, there is no firewood for the cabin and they all struggle to find some as night approaches.

III. John Butler, however, becomes lost in the deepening night and swirling snowstorm. The Search and Rescue Team is activated the next day, but even with their dogs they are unable to find a trace of him.

IV. The next fall a group of scouts from Colfield Troop 91 have a visit from a mysterious man. He replaces their consumed firewood during the night, after scaring a patrol leader who saw him in the night.

V. Mysterious sightings are soon made in states further and further away, always by people who have used their firewood. A lesson is to be learned by this story -- never consume all of your firewood or leave your campsite without replacing what you have used, especially if you do not want a visit from ''the Lost Hunter.''

THE GHOST AT SEVENOAKS

as told by Alexander Woolcott[1]

This story is a true story that happened to a young physician during an overnight stay in an eerie sixteenth century manor house in England. The story -- told to Katherine Cornell by Clemence Dane and by Katharine to me -- chronicles what, to the best of my knowledge and belief, actually befell a young English physician whom I shall call Alvan Barach, because that does not happen to be his name. It is an account of a hitherto unreported adventure he had two years ago when he went down into Kent to visit an old friend -- let us call *him* Ellery Cazalet -- who spent most of his days on the golf course and most of his nights wondering how he would ever pay the inheritance taxes on the collapsing family manor-house to which he had fallen heir.

This house was large, but now shabby, with roof-tiles of Tudor red making it cozy in the noonday sun, and a hoarse bell which, from the clock tower, had been contemptuously scattering the hours like coins ever since Henry VIII was a rosy stripling. Within, Cazalet could afford only a doddering couple to fend for him, and the once sumptuous gardens did much as they pleased

[1] From *While Rome Burns* by Alexander Woollcott. Copyright 1934 by Alexander Woollcott, renewed © 1962 by Joseph P. Hennessey. Reprinted by permission of Viking Penguin, Inc.

under the care of a single gardener. I think that I must risk giving the gardener's real name, for none I could invent would have so appropriate a flavor. It was John Scripture. He was assisted, from time to time, by an aged and lunatic father who, in his lucid intervals, would be let out from his captivity under the eaves of the lodge to putter amid the wild growth of the unkempt hedges.

The doctor was to come down when he could, with a promise of some good golf, long nights of exquisite silence, and a ghost or two thrown in if his fancy ran that way. It was characteristic of the doctor's humor that when writing to fix the day of his arrival, he addressed his friend Cazalet as living at "The Creeps, Sevenoaks, Kent."

When he arrived, it was to find that his host was away from home and not due back until very late that night. Dr. Barach was to dine alone and not wait up. His bedroom on the ground floor was beautifully paneled from footboard to ceiling, but some misguided housekeeper, when George IV was king, had fallen upon the lovely woodwork with a can of black varnish. The dowry brought by an ancestor had been invested in a few vintage bathrooms, and one of these had been placed in what once was a prayer closet that had opened into this bedroom. There was only a candle to read by, but the light of a full moon came waveringly through the wind-stirred vines that half curtained the mullioned windows.

In this museum Dr. Barach dropped off to sleep. He did not know how long he had slept when he found himself awake again, and conscious that something was astir in the room. It took him a moment to place the movement, but at last, in a patch of moonlight, he made out a hunched figure that seemed to be sitting with a bent, engrossed head in the chair by the door. It was the hand, or rather the whole arm, that was moving, tracing a recurrent if irregular course in the air. At first the gesture was teasingly half-familiar, and then he recognized it as the one a woman makes when embroidering. There would be a hesitation as if the needle were being thrust through some taut, resistant material, and then, each time, the long, swift, sure pull of the thread.

To the startled guest, this seemed the least menacing activity he had ever heard ascribed to a ghost, but just the same he had only one idea, and that was to get out of that room with all possible dispatch!

His mind made a hasty reconnaissance. The door into the hall was out of the question, for madness lay that way. At least he would have to pass right by that weaving arm. Nor did he relish a blind plunge into the thorny shrubbery beneath his window, and a barefoot scamper across the frosty turf. Of course, there was the bathroom, but that was small comfort if he could not get out of it by another door. In a spasm of concentration, he remembered that he had seen another door. Just at the moment of this realization, he heard the comforting actual sound of a car coming up the drive, and guessed that it was his host returning. In one magnificent movement, he leaped to the floor, bounded into the bathroom, and bolted its door behind him.

The floor of the room beyond was quilted with moonlight. Wading through that he arrived breathless, but unmolested, in the corridor. Further along he could see the lamp burning in the entrance hall and hear the clatter of his host closing the front door.

As. Dr. Barach came hurrying out of the darkness to greet him, Cazalet boomed his delight at such affability to wait up so late to meet him! Famished by his long, cold ride, he proposed an immediate raid on the larder. The doctor, already sheepish at his recent panic, said nothing about his adventure with the ghost, and was for food at once.

With lighted candles held high, the foraging party descended on the food, the host discussing the merits of cold roast beef, Cheddar cheese, and milk as a midnight snack, when he stumbled over a bundle on the floor. With a cheerful curse at the old goody of the kitchen, who was always leaving something about, he bent to see what it was this time, and let out a whistle of surprise. Then by two candles held low, he and the doctor saw something they will not forget while they live. It was the body of the cook. Just the body. The head was gone. On the floor alongside lay a bloody cleaver.

"Old Scripture, by God!" Cazalet cried out, and in a flash, Dr. Barach guessed. Still clutching a candle in one hand, he dragged his companion back though the house to the room from which he had fled, motioning him to be silent, tiptoeing the final steps. That precaution was wasted, for a regiment could not have disturbed the rapt contentment of the ceremony still in progress within. The old lunatic had not left his seat by the door. Between his knees he still held the head of the woman he had killed. Scrupulously, happily, crooning at his work, he was plucking out the gray hairs one by one.

Story Outline

I. Dr. Barach looks forward to a pleasant weekend at his friend, Ellery Cazalet's manor house, called Sevenoaks. The grounds are somewhat unkempt, only a caretaker and his lunatic father are left to care for the very large grounds. An elderly couple manage the house.

II. He knows that when he arrives that his host will not be there, but he settles into his room after supper, content to be in the country. Suddenly he awakens and notices a ghostly image by the door leading out of his room.

III. The figure is making vaguely familiar motions -- which Dr. Barach finally recognizes are those of someone embroidering -- a hesitation as if the needle were being thrust through some taut, resistant material, and then the long swift pull of the thread.

IV. Dr. Barach's only thought is how to get out

of the room, for the ghost is next to the only door. It is too cold to leave by the window. He remembers the bathroom which connects to the room next door. At that moment he hears his friend's car drive up. He bounds out of bed and through the bathroom to the room next door.

V. His friend is glad to see him and they proceed to the kitchen. While in the kitchen they stumble upon the headless body of the cook.

VI. Dr. Barach now knows that the old insane gardener, Mr. Scripture, was the figure he saw in his room. He drags his host back to the room and there they see the old lunatic, sitting with the severed head of the woman between his knees, happily plucking the hairs from her scalp, one by one.

CANNIBALISM IN THE CARS

as told by Mark Twain

Introduction

A scary camp fire story by Mark Twain? Well, not really. This story would be impossible to memorize and tell the way Twain intended. But it provides us with a unique story idea. Just sit back, relax and enjoy reading this one. Then after it is over, let's discuss how we can use it for our campfire story session.

* * * * *

I visited St. Louis lately, and on my way West, after changing cars at Terre Haute, Indiana, a mild, benevolent-looking gentleman of about forty-five, or maybe fifty, came in at one of the way stations and sat down beside me. We talked together pleasantly on various subjects for an hour, perhaps, and I found him exceedingly intelligent and entertaining. When he learned that I was from Washington, he immediately began to ask questions about various public men, and about congressional affairs; and I saw very shortly that I was conversing with a man who was perfectly familiar with the ins and outs of political life at the capital, even to the ways and manners, and customs of procedure of senators and representatives in the chambers of the

national legislature. Presently two men halted near us for a single
moment, and one said to the other: "Harris, if you'll do that for
me, I'll never forget you, my boy."

My new comrade's eye lighted pleasantly. The words had
touched upon a happy memory, I thought. Then his face settled
into thoughtfulness -- almost into gloom. He turned to me and
said, "Let me tell you a story, let me give you a secret chapter
of my life -- a chapter that has never been referred to by me
since its events transpired. Listen patiently, and promise that you
will not interrupt me."

I said I would not, and he related the following strange
adventure, speaking sometimes with animation, sometimes with
melancholy, but always with feeling and earnestness.

On the nineteenth of December, 1853, I started from St.
Louis on the evening train bound for Chicago. There were only
twenty-four passengers, all told. There were no ladies and no
children. We were in excellent spirits, and pleasant acquaint-
anceships were soon formed. The journey bade fair to be a happy
one; and no individual in the party, I think, had even the vaguest
presentiment of the horrors we were soon to undergo.

At 11:00 P.M. it began to snow hard. Shortly after leaving
the small village of Welden, we entered upon that tremendous
prairie solitude that stretches its leagues on leagues of houseless
dreariness far away toward the Jubilee Settlements. The winds,
unobstructed by trees or hills, or even vagrant rocks, whistled
fiercely across the level desert, driving the falling snow before
it like spray from the crested waves of a stormy sea. The snow
was deepening fast; and we knew, by the diminished speed of
the train, that the engine was plowing through it with steadily
increasing difficulty. Indeed, it almost came to a dead halt sometimes, in the midst of great drifts that piled themselves like
colossal graves across the track. Conversation began to flag.
Cheerfulness gave place to grave concern. The possibility of
being imprisoned in the snow, on the bleak prairie, fifty miles
from any house, presented itself to every mind, and extended its
depressing influence over every spirit.

At two o'clock in the morning I was aroused out of an

uneasy slumber by the ceasing of all motion about me. The appalling truth flashed upon me instantly -- we were captives in a snowdrift! "All hands to the rescue!" Every man sprang to obey. Out into the wild night, the pitchy darkness, the billowy snow, the driving storm, every soul leaped, with the consciousness that a moment lost now might bring destruction to us all. Shovels, hands, boards -- anything, everything that could displace snow, was brought into instant requisition. It was a weird picture, that small company of frantic men fighting the banking snows, half in the blackest shadow and half in the angry light of the locomotive's reflector.

One short hour sufficed to prove the utter uselessness of our efforts. The storm barricaded the track with a dozen drifts while we dug one away. And worse than this, it was discovered that the last grand charge the engine had made upon the enemy had broken the fore-and-aft shaft of the driving wheel! With a free track before us we should still have been helpless. We entered the car wearied with labor, and very sorrowful. We gathered about the stoves, and gravely canvassed our situation. We had no provisions whatever -- in this lay our chief distress. We could not freeze, for there was a good supply of wood in the tender. This was our only comfort. The discussion ended at last in accepting the disheartening decision of the conductor, *viz.*, that it would be death for any man to attempt to travel fifty miles on foot through snow like that. We could not send for help, and even if we could it would not come. We must submit, and await, as patiently as we might, succor or starvation! I think the stoutest heart there felt a momentary chill when those words were uttered.

Within the hour conversation subsided to a low murmur here and there about the car, caught fitfully between the rising and falling of the blast; the lamps grew dim; and the majority of the castaways settled themselves among the flickering shadows to think -- to forget the present, if they could -- to sleep, if they might.

The eternal night -- it surely seemed eternal to us -- wore its lagging hours away at last, and the cold gray dawn broke in the east. As the light grew stronger the passengers began to stir and give signs of life, one after another, and each in turn pushed his slouched hat up from his forehead, stretched his stiffened limbs and glanced out of the windows upon the cheerless prospect. It was cheerless, indeed! -- not a living thing visible anywhere, not a human habitation; nothing but a vast white desert; uplifted sheets of snow drifting hither and thither before the wind -- a world of eddying flakes shutting out the firmament above.

All day we moped about the cars, saying little, thinking much. Another lingering dreary night -- and hunger.

Another dawning -- another day of silence, sadness, wasting hunger, hopeless watching for succor that could not come. A night of restless slumber, filled with dreams of feasting -- wakings distressed with the gnawings of hunger.

The fourth day came and went -- and the fifth! Five days of dreadful imprisonment! A savage hunger looked out at every eye. There was in it a sign of awful import -- the foreshadowing of a something that was vaguely shaping itself in every heart -- a something which no tongue dared yet to frame into words.

The sixth day passed -- the seventh dawned upon as gaunt and haggard and hopeless a company of men as ever stood in the shadow of death. It must out now! That thing which had been growing up in every heart was ready to leap from every lip at last! Nature had been taxed to the utmost -- she must yield. Richard H. Gaston of Minnesota, tall, cadaverous, and pale, rose up. All knew what was coming. All prepared -- every emotion, every semblance of excitement was smothered -- only a calm, thoughtful seriousness appeared in the eyes that were lately so wild.

"Gentlemen: It cannot be delayed longer! The time is at hand! We must determine which of us shall die to furnish food for the rest!"

MR. JOHN J. WILLIAMS of Illinois rose and said: "Gentlemen -- I nominate the Reverend James Sawyer of Tennessee."

MR. WM. R. ADAMS of Indiana said: "I nominate Mr. Daniel Slote of New York."

MR. SLOTE: "Gentlemen -- I desire to decline in favor of Mr. John A. Van Nostrand, Jr., of New Jersey."

MR. GASTON: "If there be no objection, the gentleman's desire will be acceded to."

Mr. Van Nostrand objecting, the resignation of Mr. Slote was rejected. The resignations of Messrs. Sawyer and Bowen were also offered, and refused upon the same grounds.

MR. A. L. BASCOM of Ohio: "I move that the nominations now close, and that the House proceed to an election by ballot."

MR. SAWYER: "Gentlemen -- I protest earnestly against these proceedings. They are, in every way, irregular and unbecoming. I must beg to move that they be dropped at once, and that we elect a chairman of the meeting and proper officers to assist him, and then we can go on with the business before us understandingly."

MR. BELL of Iowa: "Gentlemen -- I object. This is no time to stand upon forms and ceremonious observances. For more than seven days we have been without food. Every moment we lose in idle discussion increases our distress. I am satisfied with the nominations that have been made -- every gentleman present is, I believe -- and I, for one, do not see why we should not proceed at once to elect one or more of them. I wish to offer a resolution --"

MR. GASTON: "It would be objected to, and have to lie over one day under the rules, thus bringing about the very delay you wish to avoid. The gentleman from New Jersey --"

MR. VAN NOSTRAND: "Gentlemen -- I am a stranger among you; I have not sought the distinction that has been conferred upon me, and I feel a delicacy --"

MR. MORGAN of Alabama (interrupting): "I move the previous question."

The motion was carried, and futher debate shut off, of course. The motion to elect officers was passed, and under it Mr. Gaston was chosen chairman, Mr. Blake, Secretary, Messrs. Holcomb, Dyer and Baldwin a committee on nominations, and Mr. R. M. Howland, purveyor, to assist the committee in making selections.

A recess of half an hour was then taken, and some little caucusing followed. At the sound of the gavel the meeting reassembled, and the committee reported in favor of Messrs. George Ferguson of Kentucky, Lucien Herrman of Louisiana and W. Messick of Colorado as candidates. The report was accepted.

MR. ROGERS of Missouri: "Mr. President -- The report being properly before the House now, I move to amend it by substituting for the name of Mr. Herrman that of Mr. Lucius Harris of St. Louis, who is well and honorably known to us all. I do not wish to be understood as casting the least reflection upon the high character and standing of the gentleman from Louisiana -- far from it. I respect and esteem him as much as any gentleman here present possibly can; but none of us can be blind to the fact that he had lost more flesh during the week that we have lain here than any among us -- none of us can be blind to the fact that the committee has been derelict in its duty, either through negligence or a graver fault, in thus offering for our suffrages a gentleman who, however pure his own motives may be, has really less nutriment in him --''

THE CHAIR: "The gentleman from Missouri will take his seat. The Chair cannot allow the integrity of the committee to be questioned save by the regular course, under the rules. What action will the House take upon the gentleman's motion?''

MR. HALLIDAY of Virginia: "I move to further amend the report by substituting Mr. Harvey Davis of Oregon for Mr. Messick. It may be urged by gentlemen that the hardships and privations of a frontier life have rendered Mr. Davis tough; but, gentlemen, is this a time to cavil at toughness? Is this a time to be fastidious concerning trifles? Is this a time to dispute about matters of paltry significance? No, gentlemen, bulk is what we desire -- substance, weight, bulk -- these are the supreme requisites now -- not talent, not genius, not education. I insist upon my motion.''

MR. MORGAN (excitedly): "Mr. Chairman -- I do most strenuously object to this amendment. The gentleman from Oregon is old, and furthermore is bulky only in bone -- not in flesh. I ask the gentleman from Virginia if it is soup we want instead of solid sustenance? if he would delude us with shadows? if he would mock our suffering with an Oregonian specter? I ask him if he can look upon the anxious faces around him, if he can gaze into our sad eyes, if he can listen to the beating of our expectant hearts, and still thrust this famine-stricken fraud upon us? I ask him if he can think of our desolate state, of our past sorrows, of our dark future, and still unpityingly foist upon us this wreck, this ruin, this tottering swindle, this gnarled and blighted and sapless vagabond from Oregon's inhospitable shores? Never! [Applause.]''

The amendment was put to vote, after a fiery debate, and lost. Mr. Harris was substituted on the first amendment. The balloting then began. Five ballots were held without a choice. On the sixth, Mr. Harris was elected, all voting for him but himself. It was then moved that his election should be ratified by acclamation, which was lost, in consequence of his again voting against himself.

Mr. Radway moved that the House now take up the remaining candidates, and go into an election for breakfast. This was carried.

On the first ballot there was a tie, half the members favoring one candidate on account of his youth, and half favoring the other on account of his superior size. The president gave the casting vote for the latter, Mr. Messick. This decision created considerable dissatisfaction among the friends of Mr. Ferguson, the defeated candidate, and there was some talk of demanding a new ballot; but in the midst of it a motion to adjourn was carried, and the meeting broke up at once.

The preparations for supper diverted the attention of the Ferguson faction from the discussion of their grievance for a long time, and then, when they would have taken it up again, the happy announcement that Mr. Harris was ready drove all thought of it to the winds.

We improvised tables by propping up the backs of car seats, and sat down with hearts full of gratitude to the finest supper that had blessed our vision for seven torturing days. How changed we were from what we had been a few short hours before! Hopeless, sad-eyed misery, hunger, feverish anxiety, desperation, then; thankfulness, serenity, joy too deep for utterance now.

That I know was the cheeriest hour of my eventful life. The winds howled, and blew the snow wildly about our prison house, but they were powerless to distress us anymore. I liked Harris. He might have been better done, perhaps, but I am free to say that no man ever agreed with me beter than Harris, or afforded me so large a degree of satisfaction. Messick was very well, though rather high-flavored, but for genuine nutritiousness and delicacy of fiber, give me Harris. Messick had his good points -- I will not attempt to deny it, nor do I wish to do it -- but he was no more fitted for breakfast than a mummy would be, sir -- not a bit. Lean? -- why, bless me! -- and tough? Ah, he was very tough! You could not imagine it -- you could never imagine anything like it.

"Do you mean to tell me that --"

"Do not interrupt me, please. After breakfast we elected a man by the name of Walker, from Detroit, for supper. He was very good. I wrote his wife so afterward. He was worthy of all praise. I shall always remember Walker. He was a little rare, but very good. And then the next morning we had Morgan of Alabama for breakfast. He was one of the finest men I ever sat down to -- handsome, educated, refined, spoke several languages fluently -- a perfect gentleman -- he was a perfect gentleman, and singularly juicy. For supper we had that Oregon patriarch, and he *was* a fraud, there is no question about it -- old, scraggy, tough, nobody can picture the reality. I finally said, 'Gentlemen, you can do as you like, but *I* will wait for another election.' And Grimes of Illinois said, 'Gentlemen, *I* will wait also. When you elect a man that has *something* to recommend him, I shall be glad to join you again.' It soon became evident that there was general dissatisfaction with Davis of Oregon, and so, to preserve the good will that had prevailed so pleasantly since we had had Harris, an election was called, and the result of it was that Baker of Georgia was chosen. He was splendid! Well, well -- after that we had Doolittle, and Hawkins, and McElroy (there was some complaint about McElroy, because he was uncommonly short and thin), and Penrod, and two Smiths, and Bailey (Bailey had a wooden leg, which was clear loss, but he was otherwise good), and an Indian boy, and an organ-grinder and a gentleman by the name of Buckminster -- a poor stick of a vagabond that wasn't any good for company and no account for breakfast. We were glad we got him elected before relief came."

"And so the blessed relief *did* come at last?"

"Yes, it came one bright, sunny morning, just after election. John Murphy was the choice, and there never was a better, I am willing to testify; but John Murphy came home with us, in the train that came to succor us, and lived to marry the widow Harris --"

"Relict of --"

"Relict of our first choice. He married her, and is happy and respected and prosperous yet. Ah, it was like a novel, sir -- it was like a romance. This is my stopping-place, sir; I must bid you goodbye. Any time that you can make it convenient to tarry a day or two with me, I shall be glad to have you. I like you, sir; I have conceived an affection for you. I could like you as well as I liked Harris himself, sir. Good day, sir, and a pleasant journey."

He was gone. I never felt so stunned, so distressed, so bewildered in my life. But in my soul I was glad he was gone. With all his gentleness of manner and his soft voice, I shuddered whenever he turned his hungry eye upon me; and when I heard that I had achieved his perilous affection, and that I stood almost with the late Harris in his esteem, my heart fairly stood still!

I was bewildered beyond description. I did not doubt his word; I could not question a single item in a statement so stamped with the earnestness of truth as his; but its dreadful details overpowered me, and threw my thoughts into hopeless confusion. I saw the conductor looking at me. I said, "Who is that man?"

"He was a member of congress once, and a good one. But he got caught in a snowdrift in the cars, and like to have been starved to death. He got so frostbitten and frozen up generally, and used up for want of something to eat, that he was sick and out of his head two or three months afterward. He is all right now, only he is a monomaniac, and when he gets on that old subject he never stops till he has eat up the whole carload of people he talks about. He would have finished the crowd by this time, only he had to get out here. He has got their names as pat as *ABC*. When he gets them all eat up but himself, he always says: "Then the hour for the unusual election for breakfast having arrived, and there being no opposition, I was duly elected, after which, there being no objections offered, I resigned. Thus I am here.'''

I felt inexpressibly relieved to know that I had only been listening to the harmless vagaries of a madman instead of the genuine experiences of a bloodthirsty cannibal.

Epilogue

I have always delighted in the caustic way Mark Twain treats politicians. In this story he provides a spoof of how politicians would handle the macabre event of deciding who should be sacrificed during a starvation espisode on a snow bound train. While it is amusing, the confusing jargon of parliamentary procedure makes this story technically impossible to tell. But it does provide us with a rather creepy story line that we can use. I would suggest relinquishing the idea of making it a humorous account, but rather telling the story of men who were snow bound on a train for over seven days -- how they resorted to cannibalism by deciding upon a method of choosing the victim, how they drew straws and sacrificed a victim, and the ending of this story? Well, that is where, perhaps, we can get clever. Rather than the whole party being consumed, perhaps only one man is eaten -- and let it turn out that he is the only one who could have saved them. Or make his brother the engineer of the rescue train. Or have a large store of food be right under their noses, either right on the train, or very close at hand, hidden by a snow drift.

Story Outline

I. A group of men leaves by train for a journey in mid-winter.

II. The train becomes snow-bound in the night with the shaft of the drive wheel broken.

III. There is plenty of fuel, but no food aboard.

IV. Daylight comes, but no source of food or sign of civilization is to be seen.

V. Day after day passes with no help arriving.

VI. On the seventh day the starvation is beyond belief. A decision to revert to cannibalism is made. A method of choosing the victim is selected.

VII. A victim is sacrificed -- suddenly either a method of rescue becomes clear or a supply of food is found.

VIII. Or we can give up trying to improve on Mark Twain, and enjoy the story as written.

THE VAMPIRE OF CROGLIN GRANGE

as told by Augustus Hare[1]

"FISHER," said the Captain, "may sound a very plebeian name, but this family is of a very ancient lineage, and for many hundreds of years they have possessed a very curious old place in Cumberland, which bears the weird name of Croglin Grange. The great characteristic of the house is that never at any period of its very long existence has it been more than one story high, but it has a terrace from which large grounds sweep away towards the church in the hollow, and a fine distant view.

"When, in lapse of years, the Fishers outgrew Croglin Grange in family and fortune, they were wise enough not to destroy the long-standing characteristic of the place by adding another story to the house, but they went away to the south, to reside at Thorncombe near Guildford, and they rented Croglin Grange.

"They were extremely fortunate in their tenants, two brothers and a sister. They heard their praises from all quarters. To their poorer neighbors they were all that is most kind and beneficent, and their neighbors of a higher class spoke of them

---

[1] Augustus Hare was an English writer who lived from 1834 to 1903. He wrote many travel books and stories of people he had known. One of them, Captain Fisher, related this strange tale of Croglin Grange, an actual place in Cumberland, England.

as a most welcome addition to the little society of the neighborhood. On their part, the tenants were greatly delighted with their
new residence. The arrangement of the house, which would have
been a trial to many, was not so to them. In every respect Croglin
Grange was exactly suited to them.

"The winter was spent most happily by the new inmates of
Croglin Grange, who shared in all the little social pleasures of
the district, and made themselves very popular. In the following
summer there was one day which was dreadfully, annihilatingly
hot. The brothers lay under the trees with their books, for it was
too hot for any active occupation. The sister sat on the veranda
and worked, or tried to work, for in the intense sultriness of that
summer day, work was next to impossible. They dined early,
and after dinner they still sat out on the veranda, enjoying the
cool air which came with the evening, and they watched the sun
set, and the moon rise over the belt of trees which separated the
grounds from the churchyard, seeing it mount the heavens till
the whole lawn was bathed in silver light, across which the long
shadows from the shrubbery fell as if embossed, so vivid and
distinct were they.

"When they separated for the night, all retiring to their
rooms on the ground floor (for, as I said, there was no upstairs
in that house), the sister felt that the heat was still so great that
she could not sleep, and having fastened her window, she did
not close the shutters -- in that very quiet place it was not necessary
-- and, propped against the pillows, she still watched the wonderful, the marvellous beauty of that summer night. Gradually she
became aware of two lights, two lights which flickered in and
out in the belt of trees which separated the lawn from the churchyard, and, as her gaze became fixed upon them, she saw them
emerge, fixed in a dark substance, a definite ghastly something,
which seemed every moment to become nearer, increasing in
size and substance as it approached. Every now and then it was
lost for a moment in the long shadows which stretched across
the lawn from the trees, and then it emerged larger than ever,
and still coming on. As she watched it, the most uncontrollable
horror seized her. She longed to get away, but the door was close

to the window, and the door was locked on the inside, and while she was unlocking it she must be for an instant nearer to it. She longed to scream, but her voice seemed paralysed, her tongue glued to the roof of her mouth.

"Suddenly -- she could never explain why afterwards -- the terrible object seemed to turn to one side, seemed to be going round the house, not to be coming to her at all, and immediately she jumped out of bed and rushed to the door, but as she was unlocking it she heard scratch, scratch, scratch upon the window. She felt a sort of mental comfort in the knowledge that the window was securely fastened on the inside. Suddenly the scratching sound ceased, and a kind of pecking sound took its place. Then, in her agony, she became aware that the creature was unpicking the lead! The noise continued, and a diamond pane of glass fell into the room. Then a long bony finger of the creature came in and turned the handle of the window, and the window opened, and the creature came in; and it came across the room, and her terror was so great that she could not scream, and it came up to the bed, and it twisted its long, bony fingers into her hair, and it dragged her head over the side of the bed, and -- it bit her violently in the throat.

"As it bit her, her voice was released, and she screamed with all her might and main. Her brothers rushed out of their rooms, but the door was locked on the inside. A moment was lost while they got a poker and broke it open. The the creature had already escaped through the window, and the sister, bleeding violently from a wound in the throat, was lying unconscious over the side of the bed. One brother pursued the creature, which fled before him through the moonlight with gigantic strides, and eventually seemed to disappear over the wall into the churchyard. Then he rejoined his brother by the sister's bedside. She was dreadfully hurt, and her wound was a very definite one, but she was of strong disposition, not even given to romance or superstition, and when she came to herself she said, 'What has happened is most extraordinary and I am very much hurt. It seems inexplicable, but of course there is an explanation, and we must wait for it. It will turn out that a lunatic has escaped from some asylum and found his way here.' The wound healed, and she appeared to get well, but the doctor who was sent for to her would not believe that she could bear so terrible a shock so easily, and insisted that she must have change, mental and physical; so her brother took her to Switzerland.

"Being a sensible girl, when she went abroad she threw herself at once into the interests of the country she was in. She dried plants, she made sketches, she went up mountains, and, as autumn came on, she was the person who urged that they should return to Croglin Grange. 'We have taken it,' she said, 'for seven years, and we have only been there one; and we shall always find it difficult to let a house which is only one story high, so we had better return there; lunatics do not escape every day.' As she urged it, her brothers wished nothing better, and the family returned to Cumberland. From there being no upstairs in the house it was impossible to make any great change in their arrangements. The sister occupied the same room, but it is unnecessary to say she always closed the shutters, which, however, as in many old houses, always left one top pane of the window uncovered. The brothers moved, and occupied a room together, exactly opposite that of their sister, and they always kept loaded pistols in their room.

"The winter passed most peacefully and happily. In the following March, the sister was suddenly awakened by a sound she remembered only too well -- scratch, scratch, scratch upon the window, and, looking up, she saw climbed up to the topmost pane of the window, the same hideous brown shrivelled face, with glaring eyes, looking in at her. This time she screamed as loud as she could. Her brothers rushed out of their room with pistols, and out of the front door. The creature was already scudding away across the lawn. One of the brothers fired and hit it in the leg, but still with the other leg it continued to make way, scrambled over the wall into the churchyard, and seemed to disappear into a vault which belonged to a family long extinct.

"The next day the brothers summoned all the tenants of Croglin Grange, and in their presence the vault was opened. A horrible scene revealed itself. The vault was full of coffins; they had been broken open, and their contents, horribly mangled and distorted, were scattered over the floor. One coffin alone remained intact. Of that the lid had been lifted, but still lay loose upon the coffin. They raised it, and there -- brown, withered, shrivelled, mummified, but quite entire -- was the same hideous figure which had looked in at the windows of Croglin Grange, with the marks of a recent pistol shot in the leg; and they did the only thing that can lay a vampire -- they burnt it.''

Story Outline

I. Two brothers and a sister moved into an ancient manor house called Croglin Grange. It was a one story building with grounds that stretched to the old churchyard cemetery.

II. One hot summer night, the sister noted someone -- something coming from the churchyard cemetery towards the house. It came straight to her window and started scratching, (scratch, scratch, scratch) then pecking (peck, peck, peck) -- removing the lead holding the glass panes.

III. She was so terrified she could not scream. The Creature unlatched the window with his bony finger. It came across the room right up to her, twisted her hair in its bony fingers, dragged her down on the bed and bit her on the side of the neck.

IV. Her screams brought her brothers, who broke into the room, scaring the creature away. She was badly wounded, but recovered and they left the area for a short time, traveling in Switzerland.

V. Upon their return the brothers moved to the room next to her, keeping their pistols loaded. Nothing happened until March, when she awoke in horror one night, again hearing the scratch, scratch, scratch upon her window.

VI. She screamed loudly; her brothers came and chased the creature away. One brother shot it in the leg.

VII. The next day they all opened the crypt from which the creature seemed to come. There they found many coffins which had been broken open, the bodies horribly mangled. In one coffin they found the same creature, with a bullet wound in its leg.

VIII. They did the only thing which they could with a vampire, they burned it.

When telling this story, be sure to dramatize the scratch, scratch, scratch, and the peck, peck, peck. Also, the running together of the sentences as used in the text, especially when the vampire comes into the room and grabs the girl, is a very effective technique. Claiming authenticity for this story, as it has been told as a true episode by Augustus Hare's friend Captain Fisher, also lends a creepy aspect to this tale.

A MUSICAL ENIGMA

as told by Rev. C. P. Cranch

Introduction

This strange visit to an undertaker's establishment took his young employee by surprise. Frankly, I do not think that I have the courage that the undertaker in this story displayed. In this story by Rev. Cranch, we can share the surprise and fear of young William Spindles and his friends as they are paid a visit that they would never forget.

* * * * *

One chilly, windy evening in the month of December, three young men sat around a tall office-stove in Mr. Simon Shrowdwell's establishment, No. 307 Dyer Street, in the town of Boggsville.

Mr. Simon Shrowdwell was a model undertaker, about fifty years of age, and the most exemplary and polite of sextons in the old Dutch church just round the corner. He was a musical man, too, and led the choir, and sang in the choruses of oratorios that were sometimes given in the town-hall. He was a smooth-shaven, sleek man, dressed in decorous black, wore a white cravat, and looked not unlike a second-hand copy of the clergy-man. He had the fixed, pleasant expression customary to a pro-fession whose business it was to look sympathetic on grief, espe-cially in rich men's houses. Still it was a kind expression; and the rest of his features indicated that he did not lack firmness in emergencies. He had done a thriving business, and had consid-erably enlarged his store and his supply of ready-made mortuary furnishings. His rooms were spacious and neat. Rows of hand-some coffins, of various sizes, stood around the walls in shining array, some of them studded with silver-headed nails; and every-thing about the establishment looked as cheerful as the nature of his business permitted.

On this December evening Mr. Shrowdwell and his wife, whose quarters were on the floor above, happened to be out visiting some friends. His young man, William Spindles, and two of his friends who had come in to keep him company, sat by the ruddy stove, smoking their pipes, and chatting as cheerily as if these cases for the dead that surrounded them were simply ornamental panels. Gas, at that time, hadn't been introduced into the town of Boggsville; but a cheerful argand-lamp did its best to light up the shop.

Their talk was friendly and airy, about all sorts of small matters; and people who passed the street-window looked in and smiled to see the contrast between the social smoking and chatting of these youngsters, and the grim but neat proprieties of their environment.

One of the young men had smoked out his pipe, and rapped it three times on the stove, to knock out the ashes.

There was an answering knocking -- somewhere near; but it didn't seem to come from the street-door. They were a little startled, and Spindles called out: --

"Come in!"

Again came the rapping, in another part of the room.

"Come in!" roared Spindles, getting up and laying his pipe down.

The street-door slowly opened, and in glided a tall, thin man. He was a stranger. He wore a tall, broad-brimmed hat, and a long, dark, old-fashioned cloak. His eyes were sunken, his face cadaverous, his hands long and bony.

He came forward. "I wish to see Mr. Shrowdwell."

"He is out," said Spindles. "Can I do anything for you?"

"I would rather see Mr. Shrowdwell," said the stranger.

"He will not be home till late this evening. If you have any message, I can deliver it; or you will find him here in the morning."

The stranger hesitated. "Perhaps you can do it as well as Shrowdwell....I want a coffin."

"All right," said Spindles; "step this way, please. Is it for a grown person or a child? Perhaps you can find something here that will suit you. For some relative, I presume?"

"No, no, no! I have no relatives," said the stranger. Then in a hoarse whisper, *"It's for myself!"*

Spindles started back, and looked at his friends. He had been used to customers ordering coffins; but this was something new. He looked hard at the pale stranger. A queer, uncomfortable chill crept over him. As he glanced around, the lamp seemed to be burning very dimly.

"You don't mean to say you are in earnest?" he stammered. And yet, he thought, this isn't a business to joke about.... He looked at the mysterious stranger again, and said to himself: "Perhaps he's deranged -- poor man!"

Meanwhile the visitor was looking around at the rows of coffins shining gloomily in the lamplight. But he soon turned about, and said: --

"These won't do. They are not the right shape or size.... *You must measure me for one!"*

"You don't mean --" gasped Spindles. "Come, this is carrying a joke too far."

"I am not joking," said the stranger; "I never joke. I want you to take my measure.... And I want it made of a particular shape."

Spindles looked toward the stove. His companions had heard part of the conversation, and, gazing nervously at each other, they had put on their hats and overcoats, pocketed their pipes, and taken French leave.

Spindles found himself alone with the cadaverous stranger, and feeling very strange. He began to say that the gentleman had better come in the morning, when Mr. Shrowdwell was in -- Shrowdwell understood this business. But the stranger fixed his cold black eyes on him, and whispered:

"I can't wait. *You* must do it -- tonight.... Come, take my measure!"

Spindles was held by a sort of fascination, and mechanically set about taking his measure, as a tailor would have done for a coat and trousers.

"Have you finished?" said the stranger.

"Y--y--es, sir; that will do," said Spindles. "What name did you say, sir?"

"No matter about my name. I have no name. Yet I might have had one if the fates had permitted. Now for the style of the coffin I want."

And taking a pencil and card from his pocket, he made a rough draught of what he wanted. And the lines of the drawing appeared to burn in the dark like phosphorus.

"I must have a lid and hinges -- so, you see -- and a lock *on the inside*, and plenty of room for my arms."

"All r--r--ight," said Spindles; "we'll make it. But it's not exactly in our line -- to m--m--ake co--co--coffins in this style." And the youth stared at the drawing. It was for all the world like a violoncello--case.

"When can I have it?" said the stranger, paying no attention to Spindles' remark.

"Day after tomorrow, I sup--p--ose. But I -- will have to -- ask Shrowdwell -- about it."

"I want it three days from now. I'll call for it about this time Friday evening. But as you don't know me, I'll pay in advance. This will cover all expenses, I think," producing a bank-note.

"Certainly," stammered Spindles.

"I want you to be particular about the lid and the locks. I

was buried once before, you see; and this time I want to have my own way. I have one coffin but it's too small for me. I keep it under my bed, and use it for a trunk. Good evening. Friday night -- remember!''

Spindles thought there would be little danger of his forgetting it. But he didn't relish the idea of seeing him again, especially at night. "However, Shrowdwell will be here then," he thought.

When the mysterious stranger had gone, Spindles put the bank-bill in his pocket-book, paced up and down, looked out of the window, and wished Shrowdwell would come home.

"After all," he said, "it's only a crazy man. And yet what made the lamp burn so dim? And what strange raps those were before he entered! And that drawing with a phosphoric pencil! And how like a dead man he looked! Pshaw! I'll smoke another pipe."

And he sat down by the stove, with his back to the coffins. At last the town-clock struck nine, and he shut up the shop, glad to get away and go home.

Next morning he told Shrowdwell the story, handed him the bank-bill as corroboration, and showed him the drawing, the lines of which were very faint by daylight. Shrowdwell took the money gleefully, and locked it in his safe.

"What do you think of this affair, Mr. Shrowdwell?" Spindles asked.

"This is some poor deranged gentleman, Spindles. I have made coffins for deranged men -- but this is something unusual -- ha! ha! -- for a man to come and order his own coffin, and be measured for it! This is a new and interesting case, Spindles -- one that I think has never come within my experience. But let me see that drawing again. How faint it is. I must put on my specs. Why, it is nothing but a big fiddle-case -- a double-bass box. He's probably some poor distracted musician, and has taken this strange fancy into his head -- perhaps imagines himself a big fiddle -- eh, Spindles?" And he laughed softly at his own conceit. "'Pon my soul, this is a strange case -- and a fiddle-case, too -- ha! ha! But we must set about fulfilling his order."

By Friday noon the coffin of the new pattern was finished.

All the workmen were mystified about it, and nearly all cracked jokes at its queer shape. But Spindles was very grave. As the hour approached when the stranger was to call for it he became more and more agitated. He would have liked to be away, and yet his curiosity got the better of his nervousness. He asked his two friends to come in, and they agreed to do so, on Spindles' promise to go first to an oyster-saloon and order something hot to fortify their courage. They didn't say anything about this to Shrowdwell, for he was a temperance man and a sexton.

They sat around the blazing stove, all four of them, waiting for the insane man to appear. It wanted a few minutes of eight.

"What's the matter with that lamp?" said Shrowdwell. "How dim it burns! It wants oil."

"I filled it today," said Spindles.

"I feel a chill all down my back," said Barker.

"And there's that rapping again," said O'Brien.

There *was* a rapping, as if underneath the floor. Then it seemed to come from the coffins on the other side of the room; then it was at the window-panes, and at last at the door. They all looked bewildered, and thought it very strange.

Presently the street-door opened slowly. They saw no one, but heard a deep sigh.

"Pshaw, it's only the wind," said Shrowdwell, and rose to shut the door -- when right before them stood the cadaverous stranger. They were all so startled that not a word was spoken.

"I have come for my coffin," the stranger said, in a sepulchral whisper. "Is it done?"

"Yes, sir," said Shrowdwell. "It's all ready. Where shall we send it?"

"I'll take it with me," said the stranger in the same whisper. "Where is it?"

"But it's too heavy for you to carry," said the undertaker.

"That's my affair," he answered.

"Well, of course you are the best judge whether you can carry it or not. But perhaps you have a cart outside, or a porter?"

All this while the lamp had burned so dim that they couldn't see the features of the unknown. But suddenly, as he drew nearer, it flared up with a sudden blaze, as if possessed, and they saw that his face was like the face of a corpse. At the same instant an old cat which had been purring quietly by the stove -- usually the most grave and decorous of tabbies -- started up and glared, and then sprang to the farthest part of the room, her tail puffed out to twice its ordinary size.

They said nothing, but drew back and let him pass toward the strange-looking coffin. He glided toward it, and taking it under his arm, as if it were no heavier than a small basket, moved toward the door, which seemed to open of its own accord, and he vanished into the street.

"Let's follow him," said the undertaker, "and see where he's going. You know I don't believe in ghosts. I've seen too many dead bodies for that. This is some crazy gentleman, depend on it; and we ought to see that he doesn't do himself any harm. Come!"

The three young men didn't like the idea of following this stranger in the dark, whether he was living or dead. And yet they liked no better being left in the dimly-lighted room among the coffins. So they all sallied out, and caught a glimpse of the visitor just turning the corner.

They walked quickly in that direction.

"He's going to the church," said Spindles. "No, he's turn-ing toward the graveyard. See, he has gone right through the iron gate! And yet it was locked! He has disappeared among the trees!"

"We'll wait here at this corner, and watch," said Shrowdwell.

They waited fifteen or twenty minutes, but saw no more of him. They then advanced and peered through the iron railings of the cemetery. The moon was hidden in clouds, which drifted in great masses across the sky, into which rose the tall, dim church-steeple. The wind blew drearily among the leafless trees of the burial-ground. They thought they saw a dark figure moving down toward the northwest corner. They they heard some of the vault-doors creak open and shut with a heavy thud.

"Those are the tombs of the musicians," whispered the

undertaker. "I have seen several of our Music Society buried there -- two of them, you will remember, last summer. I have a lot there myself, and expect to lay bones in it someday."

Presently strange sounds were heard, seeming to come from the corner of the graveyard spoken about. They were like the confused tuning of an orchestra before a concert -- with discords and chromatic runs, up and down, from at least twenty instruments, but all muffled and pent in, as if under ground.

Yet, thought the undertaker, this may be only the wind in the trees. "I wish the moon would come out, he said, "so we could see something. Anyhow, I think it's a Christian duty to go in there, and see after that poor man. He may have taken a notion, you know, to shut himself up in his big fiddle-case, and we ought to see that he don't do himself any injury. Come, will you go?"

"Not I, thank you." "Nor I," said they all. "We are going home -- we've had enough of this."

"Very well," said the undertaker. "As you please; I'll go alone."

Mr. Shrowdwell believed in death firmly. The only resurrection he acknowledged was the resurrection of a tangible body at some far-off judgement-day. He had no fear of ghosts. But this was not so much a matter of reasoning with him, as temperament, and the constant contact with lifeless bodies.

"When a man's dead," said Shrowdwell, "He's dead, I take it. *I'll* never see a man or woman come to life again. Don't the Scriptures say, 'Dust to dust?' It's true that with the Lord nothing is impossible, and at the last day he will summon his elect to meet him in the clouds; but that's a mystery."

And yet he couldn't account for this mysterious visitor passing through the tall iron railings of the gate -- if he really *did* pass -- for after all it may have been an ocular illusion.

But he determined to go in and see what he could see. He had the key of the cemetery in his pocket. He opened the iron gate and passed in, while the other men stood at a distance. They knew the sexton was proof against spirits of all sorts, airy or liquid; and after waiting a little, they concluded to go home, for the night was cold and dreary -- and ghost or no ghost, they couldn't do much good there.

As Shrowdwell approached the northwest corner of the graveyard, he heard those singular musical sounds again. They seemed to come from the vaults and graves, but they mingled so with the rush and moaning of the wind, that he still thought he might be mistaken.

In the farthest corner there stood a large old family vault. It had belonged to a family with an Italian name, the last member of which had been buried there many years ago -- and since then had not been opened. The vines and shrubbery had grown around and over it, partly concealing it.

As he approached it, Shrowdwell observed with amazement that the door was open, and a dense phosphorescent light lit up the interior.

"Oh," he said, "the poor insane gentleman has contrived somehow to get a key to this vault, and has gone in there to commit suicide, and bury himself in his queer coffin -- and save the expense of having an undertaker. I must save him, if possible, from such a fate."

As he stood deliberating, he heard the musical sounds again. They came not only from the vault, but from all around. There was the hoarse groaning of a double-bass, answered now and then by a low muffled wail of horns and a scream of flutes, mingled with the pathetic complainings of a violin. Shrowdwell began to think he was dreaming, and rubbed his eyes and his ears to see if he were awake. After considerable turning and running up and down the scales, the instruments fell into an accompaniment to the double-bass of a Beethoven mass.

The tone was as if the air were played on the harmonic intervals of the instrument, and yet was so weirdly and so wonderfully like a human voice, that Shrowdwell felt as if he had got into some enchanted circle. As the solo drew to its conclusion, the voice that seemed to be in it broke into sobs, and ended in a deep groan.

But the undertaker summoned up his courage, and determined to probe this mystery to the bottom. Coming nearer the vault and looking in, what should he see but the big musical coffin of the cadaverous stranger lying just inside the entrance of the tomb.

The undertaker was convinced that the strange gentleman was the performer of the solo. But where was the instrument? He mustered courage to speak, and was about to offer some comforting and encouraging words. But at the first sound of his voice the lid of the musical coffin, which had been open, slammed to, so suddenly, that the sexton jumped back three feet, and came near tumbling over a tombstone behind him. At the same time the dim phosphorescent light in the vault was extinguished, and there was another groan from the double-bass in the coffin. The sexton determined to open the case. He stooped over it and listened. He thought he heard inside a sound like putting a key into a padlock. "He mustn't lock himself in," he said, and instantly wrenched open the cover.

Immediately there was a noise like the snapping of strings and the cracking of light wood -- then a strange sizzling sound -- and then a loud explosion. And the undertaker lay senseless on the ground.

Mrs. Shrowdwell waited for her husband till a late hour, but he did not return. She grew very anxious, and at last determined to put on her bonnet and shawl and step over to Mr. Spindles' boarding-house to know where he could be. That young gentleman was just about retiring, in a very nervous state, after having taken a strong nipper of brandy and water to restore his equanimity. Mrs. Shrowdwell stated her anxieties, and Spindles told her something of the occurrences of the evening. She then urged him to go at once to a police-station and obtain two or three of the town watchmen to visit the graveyard with lanterns and pistols; which, after some delay and demurring on the part of the guardians of the night, and a promise of a reward on the part of Mrs. Shrowdwell, they consented to do.

After some searching the watchmen found the vault, and in front of it poor Shrowdwell lying on his back in a senseless state. They sent for a physician, who administered some stimulants, and gradually brought him to his senses, and upon his legs. He couldn't give any clear account of the adventure. The vault door was closed, and the moonlight lay calm upon the white stones, and no sounds were heard but the wind, now softly purring among the pines and cedars.

They got him home, and, to his wife's joy, found him uninjured. He made light of the affair -- told her of the bank-note he had received for the musical coffin, and soon fell soundly asleep.

Next morning he went to his iron safe to reassure himself about the bank-note -- for he had an uncanny dream about it. To his amazement and grief it was gone, and in its place was a piece of charred paper.

The undertaker lost himself in endless speculations about this strange adventure, and began to think there was diabolical witchcraft in the whole business, after all.

One day, however, looking over the parish record, he came upon some facts with regard to the Italian family who had owned that vault. On comparing these notes with the reminiscences of one or two of the older inhabitants of Boggsville, he made out something like the following history: --

Signor Domerico Pietri, an Italian exile of noble family, had lived in that town some fifty years since. He was of an unsocial, morose disposition, and very proud. His income was small, and his only son Ludovico, who had decided musical talent, determined to seek his fortune in the larger cities, as a performer on the double-bass. It was said his execution on the harmonic notes was something marvellous. But his father opposed his course, either from motives of family pride, or wishing him to engage in commerce; and one day, during an angry dispute with him, banished him from his house.

Very little was known of Ludovico Pietri. He lived a wandering life, and suffered from poverty. Finally all trace was lost of him. the old man died, and was buried, along with other relatives, in the Italian vault.

But there was a story told of a performer on the double-bass, who played such wild, passionate music, and with such skill, that in his lonely garret, one night, the devil appeared, and offered him a great bag of gold for his big fiddle -- proposing at the same time that he should sign a contract that he would not play any more *during his lifetime* -- except at his (the fiend's) bidding. The musician, being very poor, accepted the offer and signed the contract, and the devil vanished with his big fiddle. But afterward the poor musician repented the step he had taken, and took it so to heart that he became insane and dead.

Now, whether this strange visitor to Mr. Shrowdwell's coffin establishment, who walked the earth in this unhappy frame of mind, was a live man, or the ghost of the poor maniac, was a question which could not be satisfactorily settled.

Some hopeless unbelievers said that the strange big fiddle-case was a box of nitroglycerine or fulminating powder, or an infernal machine; while others as firmly believed that there was something supernatural and uncanny about the affair, but ventured no philosophical theory in the case.

And as for the undertaker, he was such a hopeless sceptic all his life, that he at last came to the conclusion that he must have been dreaming when he had that adventure in the graveyard; and this notwithstanding William Spindles' repeated declarations, and those of the two other young men (none of whom accompanied Shrowdwell in this visit), that everything happened just as I have related it.

Story Outline

I. Young William Spindles sits amidst the coffins of Mr. Simon Shrowdwell's mortuary.

II. There is a strange knocking, the light burns low, and a man desires to be measured for an unusually shaped coffin.

III. Sprindles complies, but is scared.

IV. He pays his boss the next day and the coffin is made.

V. On Friday night the man returns with strange knocking, the light dims, but then reveals a death-like face. Even the cat is scared. He easily lifts the heavy coffin and leaves in the night.

VI. The three boys go with the brave undertaker to the cemetery, but upon hearing strange musical sounds, the boys go home rather than help investigate.

VII. The undertaker goes to the vault with the noise, the coffin slams shut. He hears the coffin being locked, but he tries to open it -- an explosion takes place.

VIII. He is found outside the closed vault. The bank-note is found charred in the safe.

IX. We are told the legend of Signor Pietri's son Ludovico signing a pact with the devil not to play during his lifetime.

X. Mr. Shrowdwell, the undertaker, decides that he must have imagined the cemetery episode, but the three young men know this story to be true.

THE HAUNTING AT VINE STREET

as told by Ambrose Bierce[1]

This story is told as actually having happened to a newspaper reporter by the name of Henry Saylor. He was a reporter for the Cincinnati Commercial. In the year 1859 a vacant house in Cincinnati on Vine Street became the center of local excitement because of the strange sights and sounds said to be observed in it nightly. According to the testimony of many reputable residents of the vicinity, there was no explanation for these activities, unless the house was haunted!

Figures with something singularly unfamiliar about them were seen by crowds on the sidewalk to pass in and out. No one could say just where they appeared on the front lawn on their way to the front door, nor at exactly what point they vanished on the way out. It should be said that each witness knew where these things happened ... it's just that no two people could agree.

Also, they all disagreed upon their description of the figures. Some of the bolder of the curious crowd ventured on several evenings to stand upon the door steps to intercept them, or to at least get a closer look at them. These courageous men, it was

---

[1] The original source for this story was *Some Haunted Houses*, a collection of true hauntings by Ambrose Bierce. This story has been altered for better ease in campfire story telling. The original title was "A Fruitless Assignment."

said, were unable to force the door by their united strength, and always were hurled from the steps by some invisible agency and even injured -- the door immediately afterward opening, apparently of its own volition, to admit or let out some ghostly guest.

The dwelling was known as the Roscoe house. A family of that name lived there once, but one by one they disappeared, the last to leave being an old woman. Stories of foul play and successive murders had always been rife, but never were authenticated.

One day during the height of the excitement, Mr. Saylor was called to the editor's office of the Commercial for orders. He received a note from the city editor which read as follows: "Go and pass the night alone in the haunted house on Vine Street and if anything occurs worth while make two columns." Saylor obeyed his superior; he could not afford to lose his position on the paper.

Telling the police of his intention, he entered the house through a rear window before dark, walked through the deserted rooms, bare of furniture, dusty and desolate, and seating himself at last in the parlor on an old sofa which he had dragged in from another room, watched the deepening of the gloom as night came on.

Before it was altogether dark, the curious crowd had collected in the street, silent, as a rule, and expectant, with here and there an unbeliever uttering his incredulity and courage with scornful remarks or ribald cries. None knew of the anxious watcher inside. He feared to make a light. The uncurtained windows would have betrayed his presence, subjecting him to insult from the crowd, possibly injury. Moreover, he was too conscientious to do anything to alter any of the customary conditions under which the manifestations were said to occur.

It was now dark outside, but light from the street faintly illuminated the part of the room that he was in. He had opened every door in the whole interior, above and below, but all of the outer ones were locked and bolted.

Sudden exclamations from the crowd caused him to spring to the window and look out! He saw the figure of a man moving rapidly across the lawn towards the building -- saw it ascend the steps; then a projection of the wall concealed it. There was a noise as of the opening and closing of the hall door; he heard quick, heavy footsteps along the passage -- heard them ascend the stairs -- heard them on the uncarpeted floor of the chamber immediately overhead!

Saylor prompty drew his pistol, and groping his way up the stairs entered the chamber, dimly lighted from the street. No one was there. He heard footsteps in an adjoining room and entered that. It was dark and silent. He struck his foot against some object on the floor, knelt by it, passed his hand over it.

It was a human head! The head of a woman! Lifting it by the hair this iron-nerved man returned to the half-lighted room below, carried it near the window and attentively examined it. While so engaged he was half conscious of the rapid opening and closing of the outer door, of foot-falls sounding all about him. He raised his eyes from the ghastly object of his attention and saw himself the center of a crowd of men and women dimly seen! The room was thronged with them. He thought the people had broken in.

"Ladies and gentlemen," he said, coolly, "you see me under suspicious circumstances, but --" his voice was drowned in peals of laughter -- such laughter as is heard in asylums for the insane.

The persons about him pointed at the object in his hand and their merriment increased as he dropped it and it went rolling among their feet. They danced about it with gestures grotesque and attitudes obscene and indescribable. They struck it with their feet, urging it about the room from wall to wall; pushed and overthrew one another in their struggles to kick it; cursed and screamed and sang snatches of ribald songs as the battered head bounded about the room as if in terror and trying to escape. At last it shot out of the door into the hall, followed by all, with tumultuous haste. That moment the door closed with a sharp concussion. Saylor was alone, in dead silence.

Carefully putting away his pistol, which all the time he had held in his hand, he went to the window and looked out. the street was deserted and silent; the lamps were extinguished; the roofs and chimneys of the houses were sharply outlined against the dawn light in the east.

He left the house, the door yielding easily to his hand, and walked to the Commercial office. The city editor was still in his office -- asleep.

Saylor waked him and said: "I have been at the haunted house."

The editor stared blankly, as if not wholly awake. "Good God!" he cried, "are you all right?"

"Yes, why not?"

The editor made no answer, but continued staring.

"I passed the night there -- it seems," said Saylor.

"They say that things were uncommonly quiet out there," the editor said, trifling with a paper-weight upon which he had dropped his eyes. "Did anything occur?"

"Why, nothing whatever."

Story Outline

I. An empty house on Vine Street in Cincinnati is reported to be haunted, with ghosts entering and leaving.

II. Henry Saylor is given the assignment by the editor of the Cincinnati Commercial to spend the night alone in the house and to write a story about it, if anything happens.

III. Saylor tells the police, then enters the house through a back window. He does not use any lights, for he doesn't want the crowd gathering in front of the house to see him and he wants to avoid disturbing anything that might be happening within.

IV. He hears a noise from the crowd, looks out the window and sees a ghostly figure enter the front of the house. He hears its footsteps go upstairs, but when he goes up there, he can find nothing.

V. He hears footsteps in the adjoining room and enters it. His foot strikes something. When he touches it he realizes that it is a human head!

VI. He carries it to the half-lighted room below to examine it. When he gets there he realizes that he is surrounded by dimly seen figures. He tries to explain what he is doing there with a human head.

VII. The figures dance around him merrily, grotesquely -- he drops the head and the figures kick it around the room.

VIII. The head bounces around the room as if in terror and trying to escape -- it is finally kicked out the door and down the hall, followed by all. He is left alone, in dead silence.

IX. He returns to the newspaper office and tells the editor that he spent the night out there. When asked if anything happened he says, ''Why, nothing whatever.''

DELUSE'S GOLDEN CURSE

as told by Ambrose Bierce[1]

Those who have labored hard for their treasures, and who have done so at the cost of selling their souls, do not part with treasure easily. Such may be the cause of the tragic events which were recorded in a haunted house near the town of Gallipolis, Ohio, in 1867.

For many years there lived close to the town of Gallipolis an old man named Herman Deluse. Very little was known of his history, for he would never speak of it himself nor encourage others to do so. It was a common belief among his neighbors that he had once been a pirate -- he would have been a young man in the early 1800's, a time in our history when pirates still frequented the coasts of the United States. He had a collection of old weapons -- boarding pikes, cutlasses, and ancient flintlock pistols that, coupled with his secret ways, caused this rumor to persist.

He lived entirely alone in a small four room house which was falling rapidly into decay and never repaired further than was required by the weather. It stood on a slight elevation in the

---

[1] The original source for this story was *Some Haunted Houses*, a collection of true hauntings by Ambrose Bierce. This story has been altered for better ease in campfire story telling. The original title was "The Isle of Pines."

midst of a large, stony field overgrown with brambles, and cultivated in patches and only in the most primitive way. It was his only visible property, but could have hardly yielded him a living, even as simple and few as were his needs. He seemed to always have ready money. He paid cash for all his purchases at the village stores roundabout, seldom buying more than two or three times at the same place until after the lapse of a considerable time. He got no commendation for this equal distribution of his patronage; people were disposed to regard it as an effort to attempt to conceal his possession of so much money. That he had great hoards of ill-gotten gold buried somewhere about his tumbledown dwelling was not reasonably to be doubted by any honest soul in his neighborhood.

On 9 November 1867, the old man died. At least his dead body was discovered on the 10th, and physicians testified that death had occurred about twenty-four hours previously -- precisely how, they were unable to say. The post-mortem examination showed every organ to be absolutely healthy, with no indication of disorder or violence. According to them, death must have taken place about noon, yet the body was found in bed. The verdict of the coroner's jury was that he ''came to his death by a visitation of God''. The body was buried and the public administrator took charge of the estate.

A rigorous search disclosed nothing more than was already known about the dead man, and much patient excavation here and there about the premises by thoughtful and thrifty neighbors went un-rewarded. The administrator locked up the house against the time when the property, real and personal, should be sold by law.

The night of 20 November was boisterous. A furious gale stormed across the country, scourging it with desolating drifts of sleet. Great trees were torn from the earth and hurled across the roads. So wild a night had never been known in all that region, but towards morning the storm had blown itself out of breath and day dawned bright and clear. At about eight o'clock that morning, the Rev. Henry Galbraith, a well-known and highly esteemed Lutheran minister, arrived on foot at his house, a mile and a half from the Deluse place. Mr. Galbraith had been away for a month in Cincinnati. He had come up the river in a steamboat, and landing at Gallipolis the previous evening had immediately obtained a horse and buggy and set out for home. The violence of the storm had delayed him over night, and in the morning the fallen trees had compelled him to abandon his horse and buggy and continue his journey on foot.

"But where did you spend the night?" inquired his wife, after he had briefly related his adventure.

"With old Deluse at the 'Isle of Pines',[2] was the laughing reply; "and a glum enough time I had of it. He made no objection to my remaining, but not a word could I get out of him."

Fortunately for the interests of truth there was present at this conversation a visitor to the reverend's house, Mr. Robert Maren, a lawyer from Columbus, Ohio. The family was astonished at what the reverend had said, for they knew old Deluse had been dead almost over two weeks. Mr. Maren, with a gesture, stopped the others from saying anything and calmly inquired: "How came you to go in there?"

This is Mr. Maren's version of Rev. Galbraith's reply:

"I saw a light moving about the house, and being nearly blinded by the sleet, and half frozen besides, drove in at the gate and put my horse in the old rail stable, where it is now.

I then rapped at the door, and getting no invitation went in without one. The room was dark, but having matches I found a candle and lit it. I tried to enter the adjoining room, but the door was solidly shut, and although I heard the old man's heavy footsteps in there he made no response to my calls.

There was no fire in the hearth, so I made one and lying down before it with my overcoat under my head, prepared myself for sleep. Pretty soon the door that I had tried silently opened and the old man came in carrying a candle. I spoke to him pleasantly, apologizing for my intrusion, but he took no notice of me.

---

[2] The Isle of Pines was once a famous rendezvous for pirates -- the Rev. Galbraith jokingly referred to Deluse's house as the Isle of Pines because of his supposed connection to pirates.

He seemed to be searching for something, though his eyes were unmoved in their sockets. I wondered if he ever walked in his sleep. He took a circuit a part of the way round the room, and went out the same way he had come in. Twice more before I slept he came back into the room, acting in precisely the same way, and departing as at first. In the intervals I heard him trampling all over the house, his footsteps distinctly audible in the pauses of the storm. When I woke in the morning, he had already gone out.''

Mr. Maren attempted some further questioning, but he was unable to any longer restrain the family's tongues. The story of Deluse's death and burial came out, greatly to the good minister's astonishment.

"The explanation of your adventure is very simple," said Mr. Maren. "I don't believe old Deluse walks in his sleep -- not in his present one; but you evidently dream in yours.''

And to this view of the matter Rev. Galbraith was compelled reluctantly to agree.

Nevertheless, a late hour of that very night found these two gentlemen, accompanied by a son of the minister, in the road in front of the old Deluse house.

There was a light inside! It appeared now at one window, now at another. The three men advanced to the door.

Just as they reached it there came from the interior a confusion of the most appalling sounds -- the clash of weapons, steel against steel, sharp explosions of firearms, shrieks of women, groans and curses of men in combat!

The investigators stood a moment, determined, but frightened. Then Rev. Galbraith tried the door. It was stuck fast. But the minister was a man of courage, a man, moreover, of tremendous strength. He retreated several steps and rushed against the door, striking it with his right shoulder and bursting it from the frame with a loud crash! In a moment the three were inside. Darkness and silence! The only sound was the beating of their hearts.

Mr. Maren had provided himself with matches and a candle.

With some difficulty, due to his excitement, he made a light. They proceeded to explore the place, passing from room to room. Everything was in orderly arrangement, as it had been left by the sheriff. Nothing had been disturbed. A light coating of dust was everywhere. A back door was partly open, as if by neglect, and their first thought was that the people making the noise had escaped through it.

The door was opened and the light of the candle shone through upon the ground! [Quicken your voice throughout this sentence for dramatic effect, then slowly utter the rest of the paragraph.] The previous night's storm had left a light coating of snow. There were no foot prints -- the white surface was unbroken.

They closed the door and entered the last room of the four that the house contained -- that farthest from the road, in an angle of the building. Here the candle in Mr. Maren's hand was suddenly extinguished as if by a draught of air!

ALMOST IMMEDIATELY FOLLOWED THE SOUND OF A HEAVY FALL! When the candle had been hastily relighted, the preacher's son was seen lying flat on the floor, a little distance from the others! He was dead!

The boy's neck had been broken by a heavy bag of gold coins, coins that were later found to be Spanish pieces of eight. Directly over the body, a board had been torn from the ceiling -- the place from where the bag had fallen!

The boy had paid the penalty for entering the haunted house. But with his death the old pirate's curse was ended, for the mysterious activities of the house were never heard again.

Story Outline

I. An old man named Deluse lived alone in a four room house near Gallipolis, Ohio. Local people thought he might have been a pirate in the old days. He always had money and was very secretive.

II. He died on 9 November 1867. People searched for his gold, but none was found. The sheriff locked the house which was to be sold at public sale later.

III. On 20 November a tremendous storm hit the area, with sleet and winds that tore down trees. The Rev. Galbraith was trying to return home, but could not. He spent the night at the Deluse house, and travelled home on foot the next day.

IV. He told his family of the strange night he had spent with Deluse not talking to him. His family was amazed for Deluse had been dead over two weeks. A friend of the family was visiting, Mr. Maren, a lawyer from Columbus, Ohio.

V. Rev. Galbraith, his son, and Mr. Maren visit the old Deluse house that night. On the front steps they hear a terrible clamor inside of fighting.

VI. Rev. Galbraith breaks the door down. They find themselves inside, but with the house empty and quiet. They can find no evidence of activity inside, or on the snowy ground when they look out the back door.

VII. They enter the fourth room. Suddenly the candle is blown out! They hear a thud! When they re-light the candle, the minister's son is dead, killed by a bag of gold that had fallen from the ceiling.

THE TALKING CORPSE

as told by Nancy Roberts[1]

Near modern day Winston-Salem, North Carolina, there is a historic settlement called Old Salem. This is a true story of a ghost that appeared in the Old Salem Tavern.

It was a bitterly cold November evening and a drizzling rain added to the discomfort of travelers. Many decided to stop early and enjoy the Tavern's cheer. As the keeper of Old Salem Tavern busily greeted new arrivals, he had not the slightest premonition that this night was to be the start of a most unusual chain of events.

It was a house of entertainment with a widespread reputation for hospitality and had often been host to distinguished visitors. George Washington himself lodged here for two days on his 1791 visit to North Carolina.

As the hour grew late the social rooms emptied, the guests retired, and the tavern keeper sat alone before his upright walnut desk. His office door opened off one side of the rear of the large tavern hall. At the left of his desk was a small window which admitted enough light to allow him to see his accounts. And at the far end of the tiny cubicle stood a tall wardrobe.

Oftentimes before he went to bed the tavern keeper would

[1] Reprinted by permission of Nancy Roberts from Ghosts of the Carolinas, McNally and Loftin, Charlotte, North Carolina, publishers, copyright 1962 by Nancy Roberts.

check his menu for the following day. As his eyes scanned the listing of mutton, venison, vegetables, kraut, cheese, and gingerbread, he thought he heard a faint rapping sound. He stepped out in the hall and listened. There was someone at the front door.

While he threw the heavy bolt the hall clock chimed half after eleven. He opened the door and a man swaggered across the threshold. A wave of irritation swept over the tavern keeper at the thought of having to deal with a drunken traveler at this hour -- and then he saw his guest's face ...

It was gray and drawn with suffering. This was no drunk. It was a desperately ill man.

The tavern keeper summoned the hostler to care for his visitor's mare, seated the man in a chair in the gentlemen's room and went to arouse his two slaves. One he sent after a doctor "with all possible haste," and the other he directed to help the sick man to his room.

The man was in such anguish that he could not even tell the tavern keeper his name. So the keeper decided to wait until morning to register him. By now the doctor had arrived. He examined the patient, administered some medication from his bag and then drew the tavern keeper to one side.

"This man is gravely ill. If he is not much improved by morning, you must call me."

Shortly afterwards the patient lapsed into a coma and before morning he was dead.

Unfortunately his clothes were not marked nor did the contents of his saddlebags reveal a single clue to his identity.

After a decent burial ceremony the Parish Graveyard received his remains and the saddlebags were placed in the office wardrobe on the bare chance that they might some day be claimed.

Several days later the innkeeper's servants began to mutter uneasily. The slaves and the hostler talked of strange goings-on in the shadowy corridors of the tavern. They were reluctant to go through the basement alone. The hostler was as jumpy as the young maid. Nervously they claimed that "something" was haunting the place.

The tavern keeper at first laughed; then he grew increasingly exasperated as he tried without success to allay the fears of his staff. Nothing he could say seemed to calm them or discourage the apprehensive glances they cast over their shoulders as they went about their work. One night one of the slaves dropped a heavy tray which he was taking to the dining room. Afterwards he swore something had followed him into the hall.

Finally, one night, while the tavern keeper was in his office struggling over his accounts, a young maid burst in upon him, pale with fright.

"Something awful is out in that hall!" she declared hysterically.

Overcome by annoyance, the tavern keeper left the maid trembling in his office and strode out into the corridor. At first it appeared to be empty. Then to his utter amazement he heard a scraping sound and a shadowy, faceless form appeared before him.

He managed to conquer his impulse to flee and heard a voice speak to him. In hollow tones the voice begged him to notify "my brother of my death." It gave the dead traveler's name and the name of a brother in Texas. Then the hall was again empty.

When he returned to his desk the tavern keeper's hands were shaking, but he grasped his pen the more firmly and began a letter to the address in Texas which the voice had given him. He described his guest and went into detail about his illness and death.

It was not long before he received an answer. The reply confirmed his guest's identity and asked that the saddlebags be forwarded to the Texas home.

The instructions of the spirit were no sooner carried out than the peculiar manifestations ceased, nor did the servants ever complain again about the tavern being haunted.

The ghost had departed as soon as his errand was accomplished. But for the rest of his life the keeper of the Old Salem Tavern told this story of "the talking corpse" and steadfastly vouched for its truth.

Story Outline

I. At the Old Salem Tavern, the innkeeper has a guest arrive, very ill, late on a stormy night.

II. The man is so ill that the tavern keeper does not try to get his name and register him.

III. The doctor gives him some medicine, but he lapses into a coma and dies before morning.

IV. His clothes and his saddlebags have no identification on them. He is buried in the local Parish graveyard and his saddlebags are kept in the office in the chance that they someday might be claimed.

V. Several days later the servants become aware of a mysterious ''something'' that was creeping around in the shadowy corridors of the tavern.

VI. The tavern keeper is upset by his servants dropping things and acting foolish, but he cannot convince them that nothing is wrong.

VII. One night a maid hysterically tells him that ''somthing awful is out in that hall!'' He rushes out to find a shadowy, faceless form which tells him to notify ''my brother of my death.''

VIII. The form gives the name of the dead traveler and the name of his brother in Texas.

IX. With a shaky hand the tavern keeper writes the brother who replies confirming his dead guest's identity and asking that his brother's things be sent to him in Texas.

X. The ghost never again returned. The innkeeper told the story of the ''talking corpse'' and steadfastly vouched for its truth for the rest of his life.

THE CREEPING QUILT

as told by Nancy Roberts[1]

Introduction

This is one of many ghost stories researched by Nancy Roberts which lend themselves to story telling -- scary story telling. The story of the quilt is most unusual in this day and time, particularly since it is based on an occurrence in Kershaw, South Carolina, which was described in part by the Columbia newspaper, The State. Perhaps a great deal of the fascination is the vulnerability one has when asleep, especially if one is sleeping under a haunted quilt!

Clouds mounted along the horizon while the sky turned an ominous, threatening yellow. All afternoon the young couple had waited for the quilt to be auctioned off. It had no planned design and most women called it a crazy quilt. Annette Larson had chosen it as a Christmas gift from her fiance. Marble top tables, massive oak beds, china, the once loved, familiar objects of a Midwest farm family went one by one to strangers.

It seemed to Annette that the auctioneer would never pick

[1] Reprinted by permission of Nancy Roberts from *South Carolina Ghosts from the Coast to the Mountains*, University of South Carolina Press, Columbia, South Carolina, publishers, copyright 1983 by University of South Carolina, originally titled "The Crazy Quilt."

up the quilt. She and John knew this was tornado weather and they ought to be heading home. A tornado in Great Plains country meant devastation for everything in its path and sometimes death also.

A patter of rain fell. Still they stayed on. John Gerber was a tall, shy young man with a kind way about him and he really wanted Annette to have her heart's desire. Finally, the auctioneer held up the beautiful coverlet. He started it off at ten dollars. John bid fifteen. "Twenty," came a voice from the crowd. "Twenty-five," called out John. "Thirty," signaled another bidder.

"Will anyone give me thirty-five for this fine quilt sure to bring happiness to the marriage bed?" The auctioneer smiled and waited. John raised a finger and the quilt was his.

"It is very beautiful," said the young Amishman admiringly before he handed it to Annette. The quilt was a multitude of brilliant colors. Now, it would be hers forever. Gusts of wind began to whip her skirt about her legs and even before they reached the buggy, rain poured. Annette's hair clung in long, wet tendrils about her face. Gerber whipped the horses and off they galloped at a mad pace through the deluge. The girl grew ever more pale as the wind rocked the buggy relentlessly.

The sound of the wind increased until it became a roar and suddenly there was a horrendous jolt. John Gerber felt his wagon lift off the ground and sail through the air. Seconds stretched into an eternity. Then he lost consciousness. When he recovered he was lying on the ground and all was deathly still. Amazed that he seemed unhurt, he picked himself up and looked for Annette.

At first all he saw were bits and pieces of the wagon and a tiny shred of her shawl. Why had they not left earlier? Then, perhaps, a hundred feet away he saw the brightly colored quilt. He walked over to where it lay upon the ground stretched out almost as neatly as if it had been placed upon a bed. Dazed as he was, he could not help but notice its beauty. Then, he realized something was beneath it.

With a sense of terrible dread, he lifted a corner and exposed a lovely, still face. Tenderly he turned down the bright coverlet and knelt beside his fiancée. One small, bruised hand clung tightly to the edge of the quilt. He called her name, finally shook her in an almost fierce gesture of rebellion, then cradled her body against him only to have her head fall limply back. The girl so soon to have been his bride was dead.

It was 1955 when Dora Monroe and her husband of Kershaw, South Carolina, moved into the handsome old house on Matson Street. A midwestern family had once lived there briefly, then moved; others had come and gone. Dora Monroe was one of those admirable women who pride themselves on meticulous housekeeping and the first thing she did was to give the place a thorough cleaning. When the rooms were painted and the floors refinished and polished to her satisfaction, she decided on the first cool day to straighten the attic. She had left one end of it untouched at the time of the move.

What a sight it was! There were nuts cached by squirrels, rat droppings, cobwebs hanging from the rafters and crumbling old newspapers along with remnants of broken toys. She was almost through when way back in a dark corner almost hidden under the eaves she spied something. It was a large cardboard box and filled with curiosity she tugged it out. A cloud of dust rose as she lifted the lid.

Removing a layer of tissue paper, Dora Monroe was amazed to find one of the most beautiful, handmade quilts she had ever seen. It was well over a hundred years old. A kaleidoscope of colors and in almost perfect condition she immediately visualized it upon her guest room bed.

A few months later, before her daughter Florence Delafosse arrived for the summer, she thought of the quilt and spread it over her bed. Her neighbors, Nancy McCue and Anne Fraser, looked at it with mingled admiration and envy.

Florence arrived to visit her mother the first day of May. After hugging her mother, chatting for awhile, and unpacking only her most needed toilet articles she retired. It was after midnight when she awoke certain that her mother must be pulling the covers up around her shoulders as she had done when Florence was a child. But when she called out, "Mother?" in the darkness, there was no answer and she supposed that her mother had left.

Dozing off, Florence was again awakened, this time by tugging motions on the quilt, and reaching down she attempted to pull it back over her. She was frightened but stubbornly continued to clutch the coverlet and soon it became a tug-of-war in the pitch black bedroom. There was a stronger than usual jerk and she heard the hollow, spectral voice of a woman close to the bed.

"Give me back my quilt. It's my Christmas gift," said the voice. "Give it back now, or you will be sorry!"

Suddenly, she fell back in bed. The tug at the other end had ceased abruptly. Convinced that she had experienced a most extraordinary nightmare owing to fatigue from her trip, she fell into a restless slumber. The following morning the incident seemed too bizarre to relate to her mother.

A few nights later as she lay awake unable to sleep, she thought she felt the quilt move. At first it was imperceptible. Suddenly, there was a convulsive wriggling and it slithered up around her shoulders and neck. Before she could move, the quilt with a whiplike movement threw itself over her face. Panic stricken, Florence leaped from her bed. She turned on the hurricane lamp on the bedside table and settled herself in a chair in the corner of the room. The quilt lay on the bed in a pile where she had thrown it. She soon felt ridiculous. How could there be anything threatening about a blanket? She gradually became drowsy and was almost asleep when the hall clock struck two. Rousing herself she was ready to return to bed when ever so gently the triangles and squares began to ripple and undulate. As she stared in amazement the quilt crept toward the head of the bed, straightened itself out and covered it as smoothly as if it had never been occupied.

At that moment she heard a soft knock on her bedroom door and she opened it with the grateful thought that it was her mother. Instead Florence saw the tall figure of a man. He wore a straw farmer's hat and as he reached for her a dank, putrid odor became almost overpowering. From the outstretched arms her terrified gaze traveled upward to the man's face and when she looked under the broad brim of the hat she nearly fainted. The figure standing before her had a face so bruised and discolored that it scarcely appeared human.

Somehow she was able to slam the door and lock it expecting to hear pounding on the other side at any moment. Her heart thudded wildly and the room grew dark around her.

When morning arrived Florence found herself lying across the bed with the quilt neatly folded beside the door. She never slept under it again. Her fear of the quilt's being even in the same house with her became a phobia, and after relating the strange events to her mother she was somewhat relieved. Nevertheless, they both knew they would feel easier when the quilt was out of the house.

What to do with it became something of a problem. Mrs. Monroe preferred to tell herself that her daughter had arrived in an overwrought state and that the more bizarre events in her story were simply imagined. On the other hand, she was too knowledgeable a woman to give the quilt to a friend in a town as small as Kershaw for if ... and at this point she would not allow herself to think further.

Several times she considered burning the quilt but when she went to the linen closet to take it out, the bright colors almost seemed to glow in the dim light. She was not able to destroy it. One afternoon a young Midwesterner named Alfred Hansen stopped by for a few hours on his way to the South Carolina coast.

The conversation turned to antiques and on an impulse Mrs. Monroe brought out the quilt for him to see. He admired it profusely. She was aware of Florence's agitation. Her face became flushed, her breath quickened, and she left the room. Her mother determined the quilt must go. Hansen was overwhelmed but Mrs. Monroe recalled his helping Florence out of the water when she had ventured too far the summer before. She urged him to accept the quilt.

From the start he had been tempted to give in for he was greatly taken with it and had only protested out of courtesy and surprise. By the time he was ready to leave Mrs. Monroe had prevailed.

Several months later a letter arrived for her. Her face grew pale as she read it. She handed it to Florence.

December 24, 1954

Dear Mrs. Monroe:

Since I visited your home some most unusual events have occurred. In fact, had I not recently been checked by a physician, I would be even more concerned over my present illness. The doctor, a new friend of mine, impresses one at first as a tall, gaunt almost rough sort of fellow, but he has been very kind and reassuring.

Under normal circumstances I would most certainly begin this letter by thanking you for your generous gift of the quilt I so admired. At the moment it is difficult for me to do so. Indeed, you may be surprised to learn I have even considered some means of destroying your gift! Now, please do not take offense, for I do not mean that in any ungrateful way.

I have slept with the quilt over my bed almost every night that I am able. Although, sometimes when I awaken in the morning I am weak with fatigue and drenched with perspiration. I am convinced that I often wrestle with it all night long! Does that astound you? A quilt that moves?

Yes, that is what I believe I've seen. I am wondering if it does not have an existence of its own. This probably sounds foolish to you. Of course, I had to describe my quilt to Dr. Gerber and showed it to him. When he saw it all he could say was an admiring, "Ya, it is very beautiful."

The poor man was so enamored of it that I even considered giving it to him. But for some reason, victory over this quilt has become something of an obsession with me and I swear, although it may sound absurd, that I shall come out on top. A little pun, eh!

Well, perhaps, you will bear with my wanderings. I am not feeling well tonight and have just called Dr. Gerber who will be here soon. Actually, I humored the good man telling him that if anything happened to me, my housekeeper has been told that he is to have the quilt. He laughed, saying that my illness was certainly not fatal.

Please forgive the smudge on the paper. As I wrote, the light in my room went out. Now, I have gotten it back on. And, where is the quilt at the moment? It is on my bed, of course, and I have it just over my knees. No, this should prove to you that it *can* move. It is now almost up to my neck ... My God!

And there the letter to Mrs. Monroe ended. Enclosed was a brief note.

I am forwarding Hansen's letter to you written just before his attack. Undoubtedly, his hallucinations resulted in the unconscious state in which I found him. At my recommendation he has left for a rest and change of scene. He insisted on giving me his quilt which, pathetically enough, the poor fellow believes to have been a factor in his illness.

Respectfully,
John Gerber

The letters of the signature were tall and flowing. Dora Monroe sat down and wrote to Alfred Hansen. Three months passed and there was still no reply. She decided to phone and discovered Hansen's telephone had been disconnected. On impulse she asked the operator for the number of Dr. John Gerber.

"We have a Hans Gerber and a Eugene Gerber. Could it be one of those?"

"No."

"Well, madam, I'm checking.... I don't find that we've ever had a listing for a Dr. John Gerber."

Story Outline

I. John Gerber's betrothed Annette is thrilled at the sight of a beautiful quilt and John buys it for her at an outdoor auction as a terrible storm approaches.

II. The young Amish couple are caught by a tornado on their way home and Annette is killed, her body covered by the quilt.

III. In 1955 Dora Monroe moves into a house recently vacated by midwesterners -- and in her attic she finds the quilt which she places in the guest room closet.

IV. Her daughter comes for a visit and sleeps with the quilt on her bed. She awakes in the night with it tugging on her bed -- and a woman's voice demanding that it be given back! She thinks that she is having a nightmare.

V. A few nights later she is having trouble sleeping, when again the quilt moves. She jumps out of bed and just sits in a chair, when there comes a knock at her bedroom door.

VI. A man is there who smells of a dank, putrid odor. He reaches out towards her and she slams the door. She is terrified. The next morning she tells her mother all about the creeping quilt.

VII. They decide to get rid of it, but they are afraid to give it to someone in their town. They can not believe it is haunted, but what if it is?

VIII. A visitor comes whom the mother shows the quilt. When he admires it, she insists on giving it to him.

IX. The admirer soon writes a letter to Mrs. Monroe telling her that he feels that the quilt moves on his bed. He has a doctor who has been treating him.

X. The obsession deepens, even while writing the letter, and the quilt creeps up to his neck. The letter is finished by the doctor, a John Gerber, who states that the quilt has been given to him and that their friend has gone on a rest trip.

XI. Their friend never returns from his trip. Upon checking with the long distance operator, they can find no listing for a Dr. John Gerber.

THE INDIAN CHIEF'S WAIT

as told by Doc Forgey

There is a legend about a great Cherokee Indian Chief who lived many years ago in what is now called The Great Smokey Mountains. He had led his people wisely for many years, through many troubled times, and then finally in a time of great plenty. But he was growing old and knew that it would soon be time to find his replacement as War Chief over all of the Cherokee.

He had a nephew named Falling Rock who had found great favor with him. The young man was clever, he was strong and skilled, perhaps as important, he was kind and considerate. But he was an unproven brave who had never been tested in battle, he had no credentials that would allow the chief to place him above any of the other young warriors without drawing criticism that he was simply choosing his nephew.

The old chief decided he would design a test for all of the warriors. He knew that his nephew would try hard to win the War Chief position and that he would probably have the best chance of anyone, if a fair test could be arranged.

He meditated long and hard about what sort of test he should conduct. He wanted it to test all of the skill, stamina, drive, and ability of each of the warriors volunteering for it. Finally, he decided upon a plan.

He assembled all of the warriors one spring day on a bluff

looking out over the mountains stretching towards the west. With his back to the west, he addressed the assembled warriors: ''You braves are among the best that our nation has ever reared. From among your number your next War Chief will be chosen. Who it will be is up to you, for I am challenging you to a test.''

''This test has no end, but each of you must decide when you have had enough. It will require all of your skills. Perhaps you will learn many things and see much during your test. What I command for you to do is to travel west, beyond the distance that any of us has ever gone. See what wonders there are and bring us back a totem so that we may see how far you have gone. He who can go the furthest and who can return, he shall I name the War Chief of the Cherokee.''

The braves painted themselves as if for a war party, took their hunting equipment, and each left on his separate way -- towards the unknown west.

Several months passed and the first of the braves started returning. These braves brought leaves from western Tennessee and tales of encounters with their neighboring tribes. Finally a brave came back with the skin of a channel catfish and the story of having seen a great river, the Mississippi.

But the old chief sat by the edge of the bluff, watching with great expectation for his nephew.

Fall turned to winter and another of the great braves returned. He brought the skin of an animal they had never seen, a prairie dog, and told tales of grass lands that stretched as far as the eyes could see. He had many adventures with tribes along the way and had survived by his great skill and cunning. The members of the tribe thought that surely the chief would pick him as his replacement.

But still the old chief sat by the edge of the bluff, watching for his nephew.

Winter came with a fury and the tribe worried about the old chief's health. He sat bundled in heavy robes, staring into the drifting snow clouds, watching always for his nephew.

Out of a storm one day a figure approached. It was another of the braves who had stories to tell of another and greater mountain range to the west, that which we now call the Rocky Mountains. He had stories of tremendous numbers of beaver in the streams, of magnificent elk, and he brought back the teeth of a grizzly bear.

Surely no one could go further than that! The tribe expected this brave to be named War Chief. But the old chief refused to give up his hope. He continued to sit by the bluff's edge, watching for his nephew.

An entire summer passed and the tribe grew impatient. They wanted the failing chief to pass this title on to a younger and more powerful warrior. Had not one such warrior distinguished himself far beyond the others and lived to tell the tales of great and distant lands? But the chief was steadfast in his hope for his nephew's return, so he watched from the bluff for a distant glimmer of his homecoming.

The tribe would have said more, but the old chief was dearly loved, and they did not want to disturb him in his sorrow. Finally even he had to admit that his nephew may have been killed or otherwise prevented from returning to them. He named the last of the returning warriors as the new War Chief, but he vowed to keep up the vigil on the bluff, watching for his nephew -- never entirely giving up hope.

The old chief's health failed during the following winter. As he lay dying, the members of his tribe drew around him, mournful because of his condition. The new War Chief cradled him in his arms. With his dying breath, the old chief asked for a last request, that the tribe swear him an oath. The new War Chief, speaking for the entire tribe, made his vow.

The old chief made them swear that from that day on they should keep a vigil, watching for his nephew. The War Chief and the people, in respect for this great chief whom they loved so much, swore that they would.

And that is the reason, that to this very day, as one drives through the Great Smokey Mountains, one sees signs everywhere reminding us all to "Watch for Falling Rock."

Epilogue

Well, not exactly a scary story. This is certainly suitable for cub scout aged youngsters -- and as a humorous change of pace for older kids as well. Having a reputation as a story teller, I am sometimes requested to tell a story to a group of children, obviously too young or immature to handle the scary fare of which this book is composed. Having a few stories of the above type in one's repertoire can be a life saver in those circumstances. I originally heard the above story at a scout campfire in North Carolina in 1965. Similar stories may be found in the books listed in Appendix I.

Story Outline

I. An old Cherokee Indian Chief knows that he must appoint a new War Chief for his tribe. He would like to appoint his nephew, Falling Rock, but he knows that he must construct a fair method of allowing all of the braves to show their ability.

II. He sends them on a quest to the West, instructing them to return when they feel they have gone far enough -- the one who travels the furthest will be named War Chief of the Cherokee.

III. One by one the braves return, bringing items from distant places (leaves from western Tennessee, channel catfish skin from the Mississippi, prairie dog skin, teeth of a grizzly bear from the Rocky Mountains). Each time the old man continues to watch for his nephew.

IV. Finally, his health fails entirely. As he lays dying, he has the new chief and the people swear to keep a vigil for his nephew. And that is the reason, that to this very day, as one drives through the Great Smokey Mountains, one sees signs everywhere reminding us all to "Watch for Falling Rock."

Appendix

Books with Campfire Program Hints

Berger, H.J., *Program Activities for Camps*, Burgess Publishing Company, Minneapolis, 1969.

Chase, R., *American Folk Tales and Songs*, Dover Publications, New York, 1971.

Ford, P.M., *Informal Recreation Activities: A Leader's Guide*, American Camping Association, Martinsville, Ind., 1977.

Hammett, C.T. and Musselman, V., *The Camp Program Book*, Association Press, New York, 1951.

Hansen, R., *Camp Program Ideas*, San Diego State University, San Diego, 1977.

Pearse, J., *Campfire Programs*, Camp Tawingo Publications, Huntsville, Ontario, 1980.

Tillman, A. and R., *The Program Book for Recreation Professionals*, National Press Books, Palo Alto, 1973.

The Athletic Institute, *The Recreation Program*, Chicago, 1963.

Source Books for Campfire Stories

Bauer, C.F., *Handbook for Storytellers*, American Library Association, Chicago, 1977.

Eisenberg, H & L., *Skits, Stunts and Stories*, Association Press, New York, 1955.

Ledlie, J.A., and Holbein, F.W., *Camp Counsellor's Manual*, Association
    Press, New York 1958.

Lotz, M., and Monahan, D., *Twenty Tepee Tales*, Association Press,
    New York, 1950.

Kelsey, A.G., *Seven Minute Stories for Church and Home*, Abingdon Press,
    New York, 1958.

Roberts, L., Folk Tales of the Southern Mountains, Council of the Southern
    Mountains, Inc., Box 2307, Berea, Kentucky, 1958.

Roberts, N., *Ghosts and Specters of the Old South*, Sandlapper Publishing Co.,
    Box 1932, Orangeburg, South Carolina, 1984.

Roberts, N., *South Carolina Ghosts*, University of South Carolina Press,
    Columbia, South Carolina, 1983.

Seton, J.M., *Trail & Campfire Stories*, Seton Village Press, Santa Fe,
    New Mexico, 1967.

Thurston, L.A., *Good Times Around the Campfire*, Association Press,
    New York, 1967.

Ward, J.S., *Tajar Tales*, American Camping Association, Martinsville,
    Indiana, 1967.

Weatherby, H., *Tales the Totem Tells*, Macmillan Company, Toronto, 1944.

"AND WHAT IS DEATH? ...

Do you know it?" "Ey! I know it," answered the old Negro woman. "...Hit's er shadder en er darkness....En dat shadder en darkness hit comes drappin' down on yer, creepin' up on yer; hit gits hol 'er yo' feet. Den hit slips up ter yer knees, den hit slips up, up twel hit gits ter yo' breas'. Dat reap-hook hit gi's er wrench ter de breaf er you' mouf, en dar! Yer gone, caze yer breaf, hit's yer soul!"

-------- Eli Shepard

THE CAMPFIRE SERIES

CAMPFIRE STORIES, VOL. 3

MORE Things that go bump in the night

by William W. Forgey, M.D.

Do you want to tell something really scary? Better yet, do you want to attract the creepy things of the forest to your campfire? Augment the sense of adventure in your group. Heighten their awareness of the night surroundings. Make the kids glad there is an adult around.

Eighteen tales which range from ancient times to modern, from the deep south to the far north, but always with a theme that will leave your campers spell-bound. Each story has a moral that will entertain and teach a lesson.

The third book in a trilogy by "Doc" Forgey which includes **Campfire Stories, Vol. 1 and Campfire Tales, Vol. 2**. These stories are ideal for campers ages 11 through 16 and for adults who occasionally hear things that go bump in the night.

About the Author:
Dr. William "Doc" Forgey is the author of many stories designed for easy storytelling around a campfire. And the stories are meant to be the scary type the kids crave. He acquired his storytelling reputation during his twenty years as a scout leader.

$11.95 paperback
$16.50 Canada
15 line cartoons
160 pages
ISBN 1-57034-018-8